RESERVOIR

MAN

L. J. AMBROSIO

Best parts
114, 116

- Short, choppy sentences
- unnecessary sentences
- overuse of the word "great"
- mixed tenses
- too many superlatives

Dedicated to

My dynamic children, my friends.

A
RESERVOIR
MAN

CHAPTER ONE

1947-1951

Michael was born on February 20th, 1947. His father, Andy, was Italian, his mother, Frances, Polish. ~~Frances and Andy~~ They were the radiance of love. The day of Michael's birth they were standing in Saint Mary's hospital in Brooklyn looking at the babies in the maternity ward, but instead of being filled with joy and excitement, their faces were worn with fear and sadness. For many long minutes, Frances had been quietly weeping as Andy held her tenderly, their eyes fixed on the hole in their son's lip.

Suddenly, the doctor approached them, looking very content.

"Thank God," he said, his voice echoing in the hallway, "Your baby did not have a cleft palate. It was only a hair lip." harelip

Andy glared at the doctor but said nothing. Behind his silence was a man of great strength. He was a professional boxer, winning all sixty of his matches, less an eye. Andy's eye had a detached retina; it happened during one of his last fights. Andy had known the feeling of having a defect. He struggled with the thought of his son, deformed, in a society where perfection was the keynote of success.

Frances was noticeably quiet, loving, and sensitive. Frances had all the ingredients of a strong Polish woman. She was extremely loyal to Andy despite many friends and family telling her not to marry him.

They would ask her, "How could a man with one eye provide for a family?"

Her love was so strong and pure no one swayed her feelings toward him. Andy was extremely intelligent for a young man with only a third-grade education. He had many names: Andrew, Vesuviano (after the mountain from his mother's hometown in Italy), and Lazarus. Andy had risen from the dead. His mother almost had a miscarriage—therefore earning the name Lazarus. Finally, he had his boxing name, Frankie Lazari. Andy had a great following when he was in the ring. So many people wanted to help him when he married Francis. Dutch Schultz, the infamous mobster, even attended all of Andy's fights and helped him and Frances settle into their new apartment. Andy was very firm that he wanted to maintain an Italian home.

Frances, Andy, and Michael waited in front of the emergency entrance of Saint Mary's hospital to be picked up by Andy's brother, Patty, who was visibly disturbed by Michael's condition. They had great anxiety about their family's reaction to Michael coming home.

As the car approached the gray stone apartment house, the wounded couple were ready to face the family waiting for them upstairs. Michael began crying. His cries were not that of a regular newborn baby, but a combination of whistles, snorts, and musical flaps.

As they entered the apartment, the family members slowly approached Michael. No one said, "Oh, what a beautiful baby!" but instead they all gaped as if they were seeing a circus side show.

Michael's crying never seemed to stop. It was feeding time, but there was no way those flaps can go around Frances's nipples. The nurses taught them to hold the flaps together and let the baby suck on her breast. Though Cathy, Frances' sister, had a better idea to tape the flaps together.

Cathy said, "Now the hole is gone."

Aunt Margaret, Andy's beloved sister, wanted to know how the hair lip happened. Cathy told the family it was Sally's fault! Sally, the next-door neighbor's daughter, hit Frances with a rubber ball in the stomach. The rubber ball incident became the prevailing belief of the family until each member of the family died taking this belief to their grave. Frances and Andy knew better than any of them. ~~His parents~~

~~Frances and Andy~~ interviewed many plastic surgeons to make Michael's lip cosmetically better. They understood that if it were not properly corrected, Michael would have a bad speech impediment. Finally, they found a doctor who could correct Michael's hair lip.

The procedure would take up to five separate operations. The cost was prohibitive, but ~~they~~ ~~Andy and Frances~~ had a lot of friends who wanted to help Michael.

Michael liked his two older sisters. Lisa, the younger of the two, was childlike towards Michael. She was overly protective but could not stop jiggling Michael's lips together, making a strange perverse sound. Phyllis, the older sister, was withdrawn, dealing with Michael with extreme intensity as if she were plotting how-to beat-up Sally, that girl with the ball.

Andy and Frances would always take the baby carriage down four flights of steps and walk through the neighborhood with Michael. He enjoyed the fresh air and seeing people around him. As they walked down Belmont Avenue, so many people would come up and comment how beautiful he looked. Andy and Frances knew they were being kind, but they were happy Michael got attention. There were the occasional assholes.

One day a man came up to the carriage and screamed: "This kid is a fish!"

Frances turned her back, and tears streamed down her face. Andy turned to the guy and said, "This is my son, and I am sure he is glad to meet you."

Andy could not understand how men could be so cruel, having no compassion. Frances, at the helm of the carriage, just wanted Michael to feel free being pushed down the street.

The onslaught of operations began. Michael had four in five years. The first two made him appear worse. Andy and Frances started to have doubts in the surgeon; he was graphing skin all over Michael's body, leaving large birth-like marks. Lisa was sure the surgeon was selling Michael's skin to other people. The third and fourth operation were successful, but the wear on Michael's physical appearance was very noticeable.

The fifth operation was now on the horizon. The prep work started for Michael's operation; he told his parents he did not want any more. He was tired of the hospital. Most parents would tell their child to stay with it.

"Fine, no more! You are just going to be great. I love and respect you," said Andy. This was Andy's strongest desire, to comfort his son. He survived, so will his son. Andy had the greatest dreams for Michael.

No more four story walk up. Andy bought a house for his family when Michael was four years old. It was a big house, big back yard, lots of rooms. Michael was so happy, but he was sad to leave his friends Mrs. Rosen, Mrs. Mandel, and all the other grandmas in the apartment house. He would miss turning their lights on, rolling the toilet paper, and turning on the stove on Friday nights. These ladies genuinely loved Michael and he loved them too.

CHAPTER TWO

1952-1956

Michael was so excited to begin school at his new home. In a few months, he would start Kindergarten at St. Rita's. Frances took him to the church for the first time. Michael was amazed. They had to walk down lots of steps, going very deep into the ground to get to the sanctuary. He looked straight ahead and saw a golden altar that glittered. Michael's eyes followed the dark hallways intertwining behind the altar.

The Church was built at the beginning of World War I. The congregation built the church underground because they were afraid the church would be bombed, like the way churches were in Europe during the war.

Michael and Frances sat in the church for a while. Michael looked around at all the statues and candles until he fell asleep on his mother's shoulder. This underground palace would be the sanctuary for the beginning of Michael's emotional and intellectual growth.

Michael met all his new friends on the block, but none were going to St. Rita's Roman Catholic School, as most were going to public school. The summer was about to begin, and he would have all that time to have fun.

During the third week living in the new house, Michael came down with a bad fever. His illness got worse. The doctor came to the house and had no idea what was wrong with Michael. He did numerous tests. He called the next week, telling Frances and Andy the unwelcome news that Michael had Rheumatic Fever and had to be confined to his bed for at least six months. Michael made the most of the sad news by listening to the radio, playing games, and watching Frances cook. As the summer wore on and Michael was continuously tested for the illness, Michael realized he may not be able to go to school. He was upset.

The doctor called one week before school was to start with urgent news, quickly coming to the house to meet with Andy and Frances who waited anxiously while he was trying to park his new car in the driveway. The doctor came into the house. He was embarrassed to say it was all a mistake. Michael was healthy the whole time. And just like that, he was fine. They never found out how the wrong diagnosis occurred. Most importantly, Michael could start school.

Michael and Frances were getting ready for the first day of school. Michael had his uniform on, clipped on his tie, and had a snack pale ready to [*Pail*] walk out the door. Michael forgot to say goodbye to Pepper, his cocker spaniel. He turned around and came back for that farewell. There was no doubt Michael was afraid of his first day, not knowing what to expect.

As they climbed to the second floor of the school, there was Sister Carmina, the kindergarten teacher standing at the classroom door. She appeared to have played football before she entered the order due to her stature. Michael sat in the first-row, last seat. All the girls sat upfront. Michael had a problem; he loved to talk and comment. Sister did not like this because it interfered with her concentration; no one was to talk in class.

One Friday, Michael was talking to the students around him, commenting on a piece of dirt on Sister's habit. Sister got so angry she picked the bell off her desk and threw it at Michael. She didn't mean to hit him, but she did—right in the head. Blood poured down his face. Everyone ignored the wound and class continued.

The class was on a half-day schedule. At the end of class, Michael went with the class outside with blood still streaming down his head. His mother was waiting for him, and she was shocked to see the blood on Michael's face.

Frances went to Sister Carmina who said to her, "I do not think your son will be a good student. He lacks interest and focus."

His mother
~~Frances~~ was stunned. Her son was now hell bent on failure according to the sister. No one addressed the wound on Michael's head.

At the age of 5, after the Rheumatic Fever scare, Michael was to begin his Trial by Ordeal, the protection of the lawn. Andy told Michael no one could walk on the lawn which Andy took care of with passion. Michael made lots of friends who would come over to his house to play. It was a big house and there were lots of places to hide and play.

One day, Michael caught Joey, his best friend from around the corner, running on the lawn. ~~Michael~~ told Joey not to walk on the lawn,
He

14

but Joey did not listen and continued to run all over the lawn. ~~Afterward~~ Later, Joey sat down to play his plastic guitar. Michael told him to never run on the lawn again, but Joey ignored him and continued to play his guitar. Michael came over to Joey, took his guitar, and smashed it over his head. Joey began to bleed very badly. Joey's mother ran to the house screaming at ~~Frances.~~ Frances who was terribly upset at Michael and helped Joey heal his wound.

Joey's mother asked Michel hysterically, "Why did you do this? I thought Joey was your best friend?"

Michael firmly said, "My father said to watch the lawn and protect it from it being damaged—that's why."

There you go. Michael now becomes protector of the Realm.

Michael must confront his Trial by Fire. Michael's backyard was large, it housed four separate car garages. ~~Andy and Frances~~ His Parents rented three of them out. One of the tenants was Mr. and Mrs. Kola. Mrs. Kola was always giving Frances orders to clean the front of their garage. Frances told her it was her responsibility. The arguments really upset Frances.

The Kola's lived down the block next to an empty lot, and the Carvel ice cream shop was just around the corner. Frances gave Michael money to buy his favorite ice cream, The Flying Saucer. As Michael was passing the Kola house, ~~Michael~~ he walked into the empty lot and built a small fire next to the brick lining of her house. Mrs. Kola came out and caught ~~Michael~~ him. She began screaming.

She called the fire department. They arrived at her home with three firetrucks. Michael was so excited to see all the firetrucks, and the whole block came to Mrs. Kola's house, including Frances, who was confused why Michael was with the firemen.

Mrs. Kola came up to her and said, "Your son should be put away for the sake of this community!"

The fireman had a long talk with Michael and turned him over to Frances. No more Flying Saucer and Hopalong Cassidy for a long time. Michael was more upset that he had hurt ~~Frances and Andy~~ his parents than Mrs. Kola.

Soon after this incident, Michael turned ~~6~~ six and got a new three-wheeler. What a great bike! Michael was riding up and down the driveway.

Bobby an older kid on the block, came over to Michael.

"Hey, could I look at the bike?"

Michael replied, "No, it's for kids my age."

For some reason, Bobby did not like his answer, "Oh right, this was made for you only. You are just a shit head, asshole!"

Michael never heard someone talk like that and started to push his bike up the driveway. Bobby came up to him, pushed him, and took control of the bike. He pushed ~~Michael~~ so hard ~~he~~ him Michael fell on the iron fence. The fall just missed his eye but cut his eyebrow badly. Blood ran down his face.

It was now Frances' turn to scream. Michael was rushed to the hospital and got seven stitches. While at the hospital, Michael's sister Lisa went to Bobby's house and beat Bobby up in front of his mother and brother. She did the right thing; she protected the prince and the integrity of the Realm.

Michael, now an altar boy, was serving mass every day, except Sunday. Sunday was reserved for the older altar boys since two of the Masses were High (sung in Latin) and one in Italian. Michael would get up at 5 am to serve the 6:30

Mass. He walked 5 blocks in snow, rain, cold, and hot weather.

Father Gallo always served the 6:30 mass. Father Gallo was a kind priest; he was short and fat. He looked like a human meatball standing at only 4 feet 8 inches. The biggest problem of Father Gallo was that he barely spoke English. The 6:30 Mass was the Italian Mass, in Latin and Italian. Michael loved it.

One morning Michael left home with a stomachache. Frances told Michael to stay home, but Michael could not desert Father Gallo because he was the only altar boy who would serve the 6:30 Masses. Father Gallo had a tough time with the wine and water. He did not remember that it was on the lower side of the altar. Also, who was going to ring the bell, calling the people to communion? Michael left for church.

During the Mass, Michael was getting hotter and felt dizzy. Father saw something was wrong and hurried the Mass. They left the altar. Father wanted to drive him home, but Michael knew how hard it was for Father to drive. So, he walked home.

Frances called the doctor, and it was back to the hospital for Michael! He had to have his appendix removed. The situation was bad; his appendix was about to rupture. Andy and Frances rushed him to St. Mary's hospital, Michael's old stomping grounds.

Michael lied [lay] in bed, and suddenly, three doctors and a bunch of nurses came into his room. ~~Michael had to go~~ On the gurney, Michael said in a loud voice, "I am not going. I am not doing this again!"

One bed pan flew out of his hands at the doctors, just missing them. ~~They were not happy~~. Before they finally got him on the gurney, they had seven articles, from cups to pillows, thrown at them. They got him into the operating room. The operation was successful, but they had to pump out his stomach. Michael will remember all these incidents as his Right [Rite] of Passage.

Father Gallo came to the hospital with a gift, a beautiful rosary from Italy. More importantly, Father Gallo said, "Michael can now serve on Sunday!"

What a gift! Michael came home to a great party. Frances blamed the appendix on a bag of potato chips, this story was as credible as the ball to her stomach. Even though Michael could now serve the Sunday high mass, he still served the weekday 6:30 am with Father Gallo.

The next year, Father Gallo went back to Italy. Michael was going to miss him. When Father left, Michael told him he wanted to be a Priest. Father hugged him so tight, Michael, at 9 years old, was taller than Father Gallo, but it was still a big nine hug. Michael proved his valor and loyalty to the Mass, Father Gallo, and the Realm.

Michael was a hero; and the nuns championed his tale of bravery. His friends talked of him in images of Sir Lancelot. As for the family, he was just Michael, their Prince.

Michael's brother-in-law Brian asked Michael "What do you want? Anything you want!"

Michael asked for a Derby Box. Brian took an old soda crate and an old pair of roller skates. He put the skates on the front and back of a slab of wood. Now Michael had his boxcar.

There was Michael's chariot. He hopped on and went up and down the block. On about his twentieth time, he saw a big hump. He decided to ride right over it! Michael pushed the derby box cart as hard as he could as the bump approached. Michael flew off the cart to the nearest hospital with a broken arm. When he came home, he decided to retire from the Realm for a while. He must abandon his quest and wait until he knew and understood the potential bumps in the road of his journey.

CHAPTER THREE

1957-1963

Michael still wanted to be a priest and continued to serve mass. During this time, Michael felt the things around him were flat with little or no color. Other than the Church and home, all else had little meaning. Michael knew he must find something that was as important. One day Michael found what it was: baseball and the New York Yankees!

Michael loved to play baseball at every opportunity, and he was good. He sat for hours in the family room watching every Yankees game. Here is Michael's existence: the church, the Yankees, his parents, especially Frances' cooking.

Every Saturday, he would go to work with his father at his soda company. His father packaged and made soda in a highly successful soft drink company. If Michael did not go with his father, he went with his Uncle Patty, doing electrical contracting work. He did not like it, but he was with his father or his uncle, who both had many stories to tell and bought him lots of ice cream.

Michael loved ~~Andy,~~ his father, and he felt so secure being with him. ~~He was so strong.~~ Andy was waiting for the day Michael would abandon his dream of being a priest. He was the only boy in the family, the end of the family name.

Michael's favorite stories were those of his mother and father. Frances and Andy had a football wedding (wrapped sandwiches thrown at the guests imitating footballs from a main table) with salad wine and beer to drink. Andy told Michael when they came home from their honeymoon at Niagra Falls that the wedding was still going on with lots of people still drinking and having fun at the house.

Arriving from their honeymoon, Frances was greeted at the door by Andy's mother, Catherine, whose English was limited. It was their turn to take care of Andy's mother. Frances was not happy, but she had no choice. Catherine moved in.

Catherina
~~Andy's mother~~ hated pork, so Frances made pork chops every other day. Andy's sister had to

23

come into the house to show Frances how to keep a proper (Italian) home. Catherine died one year later, but she had one last revenge on Frances—they embalmed her in Frances' bathtub.

Michael smiled at all these stories, realizing how simple things were when you had love and caring. ~~Caring was important~~. All of Michael's emotional instincts were greater than his intellectual capacity at this point. The nuns still believed he did not have any future and reminded him of that daily. Michael did not care; his greatest learning was listening to Frances and Andy's stories about life.

Michael also loved when the nuns would invite him into the convent for lunch, and he soon realized ~~over the bread rolls that~~ he had the strongest feeling that the nuns believed he was a simpleton. Still, Michael kept eating lunch with them once a week, listening to their stories.

Michael did not understand what it was to be Italian, but he knew it was important. He did not know or meet any other nationality. At this point, all Michael knew that Italian's were passionate.

Andy's niece was beautiful, so many model agencies wanted her. But Uncle Philly, her father, did not like the modeling agencies' plans for his daughter. One agent came to the house with little notice to talk to Uncle Philly. Before the modeling agent finished his first sentence, Philly took a long knife and chased the agent out of the house to the 8th Avenue Subway Station.

Then there was Cousin Virginia Frances who had only been in America for six months. She came out of those doors with a beautiful beehive. She looked a bit trashy, but she loved the style. Five years later, everyone finally noticed she still had the beehive. A few weeks later, Andy got a call from her husband at the hospital. Virginia was being operated on. They needed to scalp her head. All these years she would lacquer her hair to keep it in place, she also never washed her hair.

Michael now had a good understanding of being Italian. Passionate, family, love, and sometimes lacquer. He might have not expressed his perception this way, but he knew he was proud to be an Italian.

Michael continued to serve mass, not the 6:30 am but the 11 am high Mass. Michael was lead altar boy, which included incense, ringing the church bell and the altar bells, washing of the hands by

25

the priest, and the mixing of the water and wine. He also did funerals and weddings.

As time went on, Frances's food was starting to get the better of him. He was matching the shape of Father Gallo, but Michael was happy. Even the nuns at graduation told him how much they admired his courage; they still did not think he had it in him, academically. At home, Frances continued to cook. She was either cooking or shopping, Andy would occasionally ask Michael if he was still on track to become a priest.

Andy enrolled Michael in a private high school run by former priests. The school was ten miles from home. He had to take the elevated train, commonly called the "el" to and from school. He felt like an adult each time he went on the journey to school but did not feel that when he got to school.

The school was run like an armed prison camp. If the boys got out of line, they were beaten—really beaten. The teachers were quite different. They sure were not nun-like. His Latin teacher Mr. Darmento kept moving something in his mouth back and forth making a swishing sound. The other students thought he had cancer. One said he had no teeth, but he did. The students all But the other agreed that he had teeth, and Michael saw them ~~in his mouth~~.

Then there was Mr. Denis, who taught History. One day he stopped in mid-sentence, pausing for about three or four minutes before looking at the class and screaming, "It is a sin if you touch yourself and the seed falls! You have destroyed a life; it is a sin!" Michael had no idea what he meant. Some of the guys in the class were giggling. Mr. Denis, shouting, kicked them out of the room.

About a month later, Michael was walking home past an empty lot on his block and saw James, the bully, sitting in this old cab from a truck. James looked as if he was hitting himself hard in his stomach. Suddenly, he saw a stream of white puss shoot out. James was laughing at Michael and told him to join him in the cab. James taught him how to hit himself and have fun. He now knew what Mr. Denis was talking about, and every time he saw Mr. Denis he smiled.

Michael was liking life, and he loved nature. He would go to the park and sit under the trees. He would sit, speaking to anyone. They would tell him about their lives, especially their troubles. Michael would sit with them for hours. He would wonder how he would feel being them. There was no praying with these new friends, just caring.

One day, three men approached him and started to talk. They said they were with the Holy Name Society at Blessed Sacrament Church. "Oh boy," Michael said to himself. "That is the rich and powerful church!"

They walked down the hill together towards Michael's home. They lived a few blocks away and invited Michael in for a soda. Michael went, and they had great conversations about being Catholic.

Michael woke up on the floor very dizzy, but he did not know how he got there. They told Michael it was time to go home. They saw Michael to the door, and he got to the street. He felt something dripping down his leg.

When he got home and Frances strongly stated, "Let's eat."

Michael sat down and ate. He then took a bath. He did not tell anyone about the incident for 30 years. His butt really hurt that night.

Michael's academic achievements left a lot to be desired. His Latin teacher, Mr. Darmento, offered to help. He decided to meet Michael after school in his office. Michael was able to recite the

28

entire Catholic Mass in Latin, both the altar boys and the Priest's prayers, but Latin grammar was not getting through to Michael.

Michael sat in Mr. Darmento's office for half an hour before he came. He asked Michael to decline some nouns. Michael looked at him blankly. He asked him to sight read a little Virgil, but Michael could not do it. Mr. Darmento was getting anxious, He sat next to Michael, placing his hand on Michael's leg. Michael jumped.

Mr. Darmento yelled, "What is the problem? You are just a bad student!" His voice got angrier as he continued shouting.

Michael turned white, and then he screamed, "Steve was right, you have false teeth!"

During this excitement, Mr. Darmento's teeth fell on to Michael's lap. That ended Latin tutorage.

Michael had few friends. He remained friends with Joey, the young man who he hit in the head with his guitar. Joey and Michael loved to play stick ball. They played it right there on his block. First base was the Ford, second base the pothole, and third the pickup truck. Some mother was missing her mop, which they used as the bat.

29

The boys on the block did not exactly like Joey and Michael, but they would play with them because they were good. Joey brought a friend, Robert, who was also a skilled player. Robert had red hair. Michael was very taken by his long, wavey red hair. After the game, Joey, Robert, and Michael would head up to the cemetery and lay on the grave sites in the glorious green grass. lie.

Occasionally, Michael and Robert would go up to the cemetery without Joey. One-day, Robert took off his shirt and asked Michael to wrestle. Michael was too shy to take his shirt off but wanted to wrestle. They would wrestle for a long time. Exhausted, they would collapse with their feet still intertwined. Michael liked the feeling of being close to someone. Robert suddenly pulled away, put his shirt on, and left. Michael never saw him again. Michael would ask Joey where Robert was, but Joey would not answer.

Michael loved to sit on the bench and talk to people; hopefully, something in their stories would give him the answers to many of the strange things that happened in his life. He knew there had to be something or someone greater. Was it Jesus? He just sat on the bench and prayed. Frances would ask Michael why he would sit on the park bench.

Michael responded, "Ma, I do not know why. I do not understand. It is nice there, that is all." His mother kissed him on the head.

She kissed ~~him on the head and~~ told him he was going to ~~get sick~~ sitting there too much.

his parents
Michael came home one evening and told ~~Andy and Frances~~ he was not going to be a Priest, maybe a fireman or something. The smile on Andy's face was big. He took the whole family to the ice cream parlor. Michael did not understand why his father was so happy. He must have been afraid he would have to go to Mass a lot if he became a priest. There was a relaxed feeling in the household, taking the edge off Michael's not so great grades.

Michael's days were spent in the park. The park benches circled up a walkway to the very top of the hill. Michael slowly went from bench to bench over the course of many weeks, climbing the hill to the reservoir. His encounters got more interesting.

One day a young man approached him and sat down. He told him that we are losing our freedom to unions, welfare, taxation, and foreign aid. Combine this paragraph and the next.

31

The young man said, "We must regain our freedom and our right to choose, not the government choosing for us!"

He gave Michael a book called "Conscience of a Conservative" by Barry Goldwater. Michael had not read a book *any* except the Bible. He was excited to read it, especially since it was only 127 pages. ~~He read the whole book~~; Barry Goldwater *became* ~~was~~ a potential hero of his.

Sunday meant dinner with the whole family. Michael explained his new book and how great Barry Goldwater was. Andy, being a Democrat, explained to Michael that the man was dangerous. Michael ~~said no~~ *disagreed*, and this conversation was the first time in his life he bucked ~~Andy~~. *his Father.* Changing the subject, Michael told his family about his great quest to move from bench to bench closer to the reservoir. Frances looked concerned.

She told Michael not to go farther, "There are bad people at the reservoir." Michael kept quiet, knowing that his journey would continue.

Michael had to conquer two major problems, his grades and how sad they made his parents. Andy was called into the school; he was told by Michael's counselor that Michael could never get into a university or college. He
32

recommended Andy donate money to St. Paul's University, as Michael might attend their Junior College.

The third problem was his weight. Michael knew he was chubby and did not look presentable; he wanted to wear hip clothing. Michael went on a diet, a graham crackers and skim milk diet, and worked out heavily every night. The weight came off very rapidly. Michael was skinny in three months, and everyone said it was baby fat.

To Correcting the situation with his grades, he secretively took a blank report card from the school's office and maintained his own grading. The new grades that he posted were not outstanding, just exactly right. Frances and Andy His parents where relieved when he brought home his report card. Tension was now out of the house; and Michael could go to work with Andy and watch Friday Night Fights with him.

Michael was so close in his climb to the top bench; the reservoir was in sight. He was able to see all these men just walking around without purpose. Michael bet they had remarkable stories to tell. He was frightened because, in a few months, he knew he would be at the top of the reservoir. He started at the base of the hill, an unknowing young man. Now, he saw the top. Michael had great anticipation of some sort of catharsis. These men might have a greater knowledge. Michael only had Barry Goldwater.

He noticed there were a few men that acted strange. They must be over educated, and it affected the way they acted. ~~Michael realized that these people may have been strange, so~~ He stopped talking about them and his quest to get to the top of the reservoir during dinner. He did not want his mother to worry.

During his senior year, Michael was getting ready to graduate. In the third marking period, as in all marking periods, the students brought their report card up to the teacher and were given grades. Michael was so busy talking to his fellow classmates, he gave the fake report card to the teacher. It was the end of the world. The teacher glared at him. ~~Michael was wiped out~~. They took him to the office, called his parents, and made an appointment with them for the next day. Michael felt so bad he hurt ~~Andy and Frances~~ his parents; he saw no resolution. Michael was expelled immediately.

That night, Michael thought that maybe Barry Goldwater would help him. Set him free. He climbed out of his window, went to the Port

Authority, and bought a ticket to Washington, DC. It was two o'clock in the morning as the bus pulled out of the station.

The bus was almost empty. There was this military man sitting a few rows ahead of him. He asked Michael to come up and sit with him. Michael gleefully moved right next to him. He asked Michael lots of questions and Michael was honest. He asked Michael where he was staying.

"I haven't thought about it."

Michael was convinced Barry Goldwater would help him. The Sargent invited Michael to stay with him for a few days, and they could see Washington and have some fun. Michael thanked him but said no. Michael fell asleep on his shoulder accidentally; it felt secure.

~~Michael's father put a five-state alarm out to locate Michael. Michael could not find Barry Goldwater. He looked high and low for his office but failed to find it.~~ He made it to the Lincoln Memorial. He was exhausted wandering for eight hours. The Washington Police found him and bought him a ticket back to New York.

Though Michael looked high and low, he could not find Goldwater's office. Meanwhile

When he came through the front door, his mother was crying with his two sisters. His father

Michael's father put out a five-state alarm to locate Michael.

came over to him and hugged him to tell him it was okay.

"You're home now," Andy said.

Michael was expelled for the rest of the year and could not attend graduation. ~~Michael~~ now had lots of time to fulfil his quest to go to the top of the reservoir. Michael finally made it to the top. The reservoir was big and beautiful. The plants and grass around the reservoir were lush and green.

He was confused. For now, he saw that these men had a mission. They were trying to date one another! Michael spent the next two months going to the reservoir every day, talking to them and learning. He was innocent in his dealings with the reservoir men. Michael listened to their frustration, their aloneness, and their desperation to be accepted. They liked Michael because of all his questions.

Michael knew this was the beginning of a larger quest. Barry Goldwater, the priesthood, and the reservoir men did not have the answer, only a clue. The answer was in him. He had to go further; it was not the end of the line but only the beginning.

CHAPTER FOUR

1964-1965

Michael graduated, to the surprise of his teachers. He had no remorse skipping the graduation ceremony. He smiled as he waved goodbye to all those terrible teachers from his backyard. He had a lot of hope that college would be better.

Michael was now dragging on a cigarette—a habit he learned from his cousin on one of his family's numerous summers in Vermont. Michael put out his cigarette, pet his dog on the head, and walked into the house. Patted

Michael was sitting in his room, waiting for his parents to come home. He suddenly noticed someone standing in front of his house near the lawn. The person looked familiar. He was old, about thirty or forty, wearing a denim jacket and black chinos pants.

"It is one of my sister's boyfriends stalking her." Michael, started to watch TV, ignoring the person. *thought and*

Michael glanced out the window again, moments later, and saw the man pacing. Something did not look right. This went on for about an hour. Suddenly, the man started to come up the front steps. He was attempting to look in the windows.

Michael moved to the center of the house; he was out of sight range. The doorbell rang. Michael froze, not knowing what to do. He might be a friend of his parents, so he better answer the door. Michael quietly approached the front door; he unlocked it and cracked the door open.

The man said, "Can I come in?"

"No, I do not know you," replied Michael.

"Yes, you do," said the man, "I want to talk to you."

It hit Michael suddenly—he was a Reservoir Man. Why would he come all the way down here? Michael told him to leave. The strange man explained how he watched Michael for a month at the reservoir.

"I know your parents are not home. I saw them leave," the man stated eagerly. "It was hours ago they left," he continues. "And I just want to spend a little time talking, touching, getting to know one another."

"What does that mean?" Michael replied, nervously.

"Come on, let me in," he says as he starts to push on the door. "I know you like men."

Michael slammed the door and sprinted out the back door, jumping his neighbor's fences running toward his sister's house. He made it, exhausted, and she was home. He collected himself and knocked on the door.

She answered the door with a broad grin.

"Hey, just in time. We want to go out for ice cream. Could you watch the kids for an hour?"

~~Michael said, "No." But it was only in his head.~~ The Reservoir Man was stalking him, he could not leave his sister's home, even if he wanted to.

"Just make it an hour. Mom and Dad are coming home, and I do not want them to worry where I am."

The kids were asleep, so Michael sat at the kitchen table, looking out the open window. He still had not fully collected himself when suddenly, the Reservoir Man was peering into his sister's window. To Michael's shock, he noticed that the door to outside was also wide open. The Reservoir Man gestured for Michael to come out. Michael gathered his courage, went to the opened door, and told him to leave

"How can I leave when I came all this way for you?" he said grinning. "I want to give you some excitement."

The man moved closer to Michael through the opened door. It was now or never. Michael had to act, not just for him, but also for the kids in the house. Michael furiously responded, "I am not a homosexual,asshole, leave!"

The Reservoir Man responded, "I will hold on to you. You will be safe."

Michael was furious. He pushed the man out of the open door with all his force, and the man lost his balance with enough time for Michael to close the door and bolt the lock. The Reservoir man looked at Michael through the locked door.

"You are not coming with me? Your time growing up will be a little harder. A little more painful."

He walked away, disappearing around the corner. Michael was sweating and upset. "Why did he say that to me?" he thought. Michael knew now that these men needed to stay at the reservoir. They could not seep into his life anymore.

It is here! Michael was standing at one of the main entrances of the college, ready to run in. He opened the door with the gentleness of a Victorian scholar. Walking down a long corridor with lots of fellow students, he politely stopped one of them and showed him his class schedule.

The young man smiled. "You are three hours early for your first class. Walk down the hall, turn left, and go down the steps to the cafeteria."

Michael walked as instructed, opening the door to the cafeteria, and seeing a sea of students of all shapes and sizes just laughing, talking, and drinking coffee. Michael wandered, looking for a spot to sit.

He suddenly saw a girl curling her finger toward him, beckoning him to come over. Michael

approached her table, noticing that seven students
are sitting with her at a four-chair table. [were]

She introduces herself, "Carol, what is your
name, sweetie? You are just so cute."

Michael mumbled his name; he was very
distracted looking at Carol. She had the biggest
breasts he had ever seen; they were so big that her
breasts [they] hung over the table. Her other friends all
seemed strange. One guy kept talking about his
friends using female names.

Carol told Michael they all meet at ten
o'clock till the end of the afternoon taking shifts
going to class and, "Cutie, you are welcome here
with us."

Off to class, Michael had Speech, English,
and History! He was sitting in Speech waiting for
the professor. Then, a truly short man with a small
beard barely lifted his leg up on the podium. This
was Doctor [Dr.] O'Connor. The objective of the class, he
told them, was just to talk and express yourself. [themselves.]

"We are going to read a book for our first
assignment. You will discuss your feelings about
the main character and the plot."

The assignment was "Catcher in the Rye" by
J.D. Salinger. Michael went to the bookstore, got [and]

the book, ~~and made a promise to himself that he would read the whole book.~~ That night, he read the whole book. ~~Michael~~ He was dizzy from what he read. During his reading, Michael loved the main character Holden Caulfield and tried to find out how he related to him in his own life.

The following week was Michael's turn ~~for~~ to give his presentation. Michael was incredibly nervous, ~~he was~~ afraid the students would judge him. He got up and walked to the front of the class. ~~He started speaking with all his tru~~th. Michael explained that he and Holden had similar situations growing up. He told the class that he was expelled, a bad student, and was always searching for answers, as Holden did.

There was one thing that Holden said that hit home: "Sex is something I just do not understand. I swear to God, I do not." Michael also did not understand sex, except what James taught him in the cab of the truck. The class was stunned. The professor did not know what to say except to congratulate Michael for his honesty.

One male student asked, "Are you looking for help?"

For the next week, students huddled around Carol's table in the cafeteria, explaining to

Michael all he needed to know. His truth led to a lot of new and exciting friends. College was already much better. Thanks, Holden!

CHAPTER FIVE

1966

Michael's first semester was brilliant. His grades were a few A's and the rest B+'s, and he met so many students, some even ~~became~~ good *becoming* friends. Dr. O'Connor, his speech teacher, spent time with him, listening to Michael's quest to get into college. He told Michael he had great verbal skills but getting rid of his Brooklyn accent would be beneficial.

Dr. O'Connor taught Michael the necessity of reading other people's body language, saying, "Letting them talk first is essential. Watching their gestures and eyes is especially important. You must always talk from your head and heart; truthfulness is the most essential element of speaking."

This was the first time Michael thought about truth as an instrument of communicating. Why was it so important? He slowly understood that the truth was in him—no one knows his truth. Michael realized that all the Saints were harboring their truth as well. Saint Francis, Saint Anthony, Saint Stephen. This correlation between the Catholic Saints and himself made his search for his truth much deeper. The Saints sought a communion with God.

Michael realized his thirst for knowledge was his communion. In later life, Michael knew his communication was between his conscious and unconscious states. Dr. O'Connor helped him understand all this. His use of the Saints made O'Connor more credible since they were in a Catholic University.

Dr. O'Connor reminded Michael that most Saints died for their truth. "Now, Michael, I don't think you need to die for your truth, but you must seek it and hold it tight in your arms. Celebrate your awareness!"

Carol was still his best friend. Michael would sit at her table and smile. He never thought of having a friend with breasts as big as hers and wondered what it would be like to dance with her. "She would beat me to death," he thought. She was truly a friend!

Carol brought a new girl over to the table; she was beautiful. Carol introduced her as Claire. Michael and Claire hit it off, and he recognized her from his speech and literature classes with Dr. Rossi.

Claire had a boyfriend. She was going to break up with him because he was attracted to drag queens. Claire said he would sleep with them and fall in love for a minute, leaving Claire in left field not knowing how to deal with it. Michael was confused to say the least but found her boyfriend's story fascinating and unusual.

Michael and Claire became special friends. Their birthdays were on the same day. They both loved the movies.

Dean, a friend of Claire's, would come over to the table. ~~Michael wondered what cloud Dean rode in on getting to school. He~~ was a nice guy. ~~Dean~~ He pulled Michael aside one day and asked him if he ~~did~~ had done 'the dirty.'

Michael said in an assertive voice, "Yes, twice a day."

Dean gasped in disbelief. He asked Michael what he thought about when doing it since he

47

knew nothing about sex according to his famous class presentation.

Michael responded, "I think about doing it in front of my mother's six-foot vanity mirror."

Dean gasped, "You do it while looking at yourself?"

Michael nodded. Dean gasped again.

Claire and Michael would spend hours talking about Dr. Rossi's literature class. He spent half of the term on Thomas Mann's "Death in Venice." It is about an older man in pursuit of a younger man, Tadzio.

Though it was a very controversial book, Michael understood it was more than a homosexual tale. He asked Dr. Rossi what all of it meant. He told Michael the lead character is an artist.

Artists pursue beauty and truth as represented by Tadzio in the novel. Von Aschenbeck prepares himself to look younger so Tadzio will accept him. He exposes himself to the fires and chaos of Venice while the city is fighting the plague. His obsessive pursuit of Tadzio leads to his own death from the plague, but his last image is looking at Tadzio wading in the water while Tadzio points into the ocean.

Dr. Rossi said, "Your journey to know and embrace your reality is not easy, and it is dangerous—whether it is the embracing of beauty, like Von Aschenbeck, or the embracing of your own personal freedom."

"That is it! My freedom is what I desire," thought Michael. Once I know my truth, I am free. Dr. Rossi warned him that the thirst to know truth is often a journey through dark passages. Michael knew his difficult journey was just beginning.

Standing in line for coffee at the cafeteria, Michael felt a bump on his back, He turned and saw a young man smiling, not at him but at the room. He was a tall blond-haired person with milk-like skin. Michael could only gaze at first, but he built up his courage to introduce himself.

The young man acknowledged his gaze with a smile and a slight French accent as he spoke, "Hi, my name is Raphael. I am an exchange student from France."

Michael wanted to know him and hear his story. He wanted to be his friend. Michael would wait for Raphael in the cafeteria. Once Raphael arrived, they talked and talked. Michael introduced him to Claire and Carol; Carol flirted with him. ~~Michael had a new friend.~~ One day, Raphael stopped talking to Michael and virtually ignored him. Michael was distressed and hurt.

Claire's birthday was shared with Michael. Michael had a surprise date for her. On the train going into Manhattan, he gave her the album of "My Fair Lady" and reserved seats to see the film that day, ~~Claire was so happy.~~ making her very happy.
They both loved the film, but Claire loved it more than Michael. After the film, he took her for Chinese food at the China River on 44th Street. To Michael Chinese food only placed second to Italian macaroni; Lo Mein was the cultural compromise. Michael and Claire formed a great bond because they cared for each other.

Out of nowhere, Raphael ~~asks~~ asked Michael to hang out at his room in East Flatbush. Michael was elated. After three weeks of ignoring him, Raphael wanted to get together. Michael made it to his apartment, which was a small but nicely furnished room. Raphael said he got a bottle of wine from the French family who owned the house.

Raphael insisted they sit on the floor by his day bed. He opened the wine, and they drank.
50

Michael had so many questions for him. Raphael told him that he thinks too much.

"Yes, but I am expanding my reality," replied Michael with a smile.

Michael spent time explaining "truth" to Raphael, saying that he had not come to grips with freedom yet himself. Raphael had great admiration for Michael and his intelligence. As the evening wore on, they became more tactile, touching each other in a very innocent way. Michael looked at his watch, and it was 2 o'clock.

Raphael said, "Bedtime."

Michael got up to leave, but Raphael stood in front of him. They looked at each other for a while. Michael left. He walked slowly to his car. As Michael got into his car, he realized he should have stayed. All he wanted was to hug and be hugged. "It is getting scary inside here," Michael thought while looking in the rear-view at his own face. Inside his mind, he was afraid of the next thought. He tried to silence it all, grabbing his stomach. Afraid of his thoughts and being alone, Michael wanted to cry but heard his father saying, "Men do not cry."

When Carol and Claire saw Michael the next day, They knew something was wrong. They tried to cheer Michael up, but it did not do any good. Carol ~~knew. She~~ whispered to Michael that people from Europe are all teases.

She told Michael loudly, "If you don't smile, I am going to do the twist with you and beat you to death."

Michael smiled, knowing that she cared. Raphael never spoke to Michael except for a small 'hello.' Michael never forgot him—the smile, his tenderness, and that brief but cherished friendship.

The first year had now ended. Michael's grades were great, and he was on the honor roll. He ~~Michael~~ was sad to learn that Carol, Claire, and Dean would not be coming back for the second year. The last day of class, they had a big party in the cafeteria. Carol was shaking her breasts all over the place, and all the guys just clapped her on and on. She ~~never~~ didn't stopped.

Carol told Michael he was a special guy no matter who he loved. Dean told Michael he is now touching himself in front of his mother's mirror, ~~He must stretch a lot, but he does it~~, thanks to Michael. Claire and Michael will see each other through the summer. What a wonderful year.

52

CHAPTER SIX

1967

Michael spent much of the summer sitting outside Clean Health Dentistry on the 14th floor of the Hansen Building in downtown Brooklyn. Claire worked there, learning to be a dental assistant. That is the path she chose after leaving school. Her choice made Michael sad because he felt she was better than someone's decayed teeth.

They went for coffee after work and talked and talked. Claire ~~was changing as the summer passed. She~~ was curious about who they were together and what it meant to just "be" with one another.

One day Claire told Michael they could not spend time together much anymore because she was dating this guy, Eddie. Michael said that it was okay, figuring they could talk on the phone. That last day they were together, Claire told Michael to never stop asking questions, to keep learning to understanding people. Claire said she was sad she could not join Michael on all the paths he would take. She kissed him and walked down the subway steps saying goodbye.

She kissed him, saying goodbye and walked down the subway.

Michael's eyes welled up quickly but did not cry. He waved a huge goodbye with great force and an honest smile. He realized life will have a lot of goodbyes, but Claire and Raphael were some of the hardest goodbyes he ever said.

Michael developed a strong taste for music. Bob Dylan was his hero but so were The Bee Gees, Rolling Stones, Beach Boys, The Beatles, The Four Tops, Temptations, Ravi Shankar, and Chet Baker. He Michael formed a strong interest in the causes of Social Justice.

Michael felt strongly for the African Americans and was against the beginning of a war in Vietnam. He was taking a liking to classical music; he even went to Lincoln Center for the Bach concert. He Michael did not like opera that much— except Puccini. The only TV he watched was the new series called "Star Trek." His schedule revolved around the series. He admired the morals of most of the episodes. Michael loved life, and this

54

attitude helped carry the burden of finding himself and his freedom.

Going into his second year of college, his home environment was at its best. He would go to work with ~~Andy~~ his father on Saturday and liked every minute of being with him. He would go to Coney Island with ~~Frances~~ his mother, who loved to go on the rides. Michael was her chaperone. Michael loved knishes, and she made a point to buy them for him every time she went to the kosher butcher. Frances always said the best meats were kosher.

Their bond was beautiful. Frances still went to Wednesday night Novenas, and Michael would wait outside the church but not go in. He began to develop a strong distance with the Church for no reason that he could pinpoint. But when Frances came out, she would always tell him it would be good for him if he went to church. Michael would not answer. As they walked home, they went to the lemon ice stand. Frances and Michael would slowly walk home, savoring both their lemon ice and ~~the~~ their moments together.

As the summer was ending, Michael was looking forward to the fall semester. ~~Michael~~ He got his schedule after much anticipation. He had Mr. Rossi again for literature; ~~he was happy and looking~~

forward to his classes. A week before classes started, Michael hopped on the A train to take a self-tour of Greenwich Village. Walking around, he Michael was so tempted to sit on a bench and talk to people, but he was too nervous. He walked down to the water and finally sat on the only new bench

A young man sat within seconds right next to him. They started talking. He told Michael his name was Misha.

"I am Russian. My family came to America," said Misha.

He told Michael his family was rich in Russia, but the Russian Government took all their money. Michael did not know what to say other than this guy was a liar. He had no Russian accent, dressed in drab worn clothing, and kept rearranging his privates. They talked for a long time, and as the time passed, Michael thought increasingly about how many lies one person could say in a brief period. Somehow, Michael liked him. Misha told Michael to come meet his friends because they were having a small party on Friday at the Hotel Albert in the Village, and he insisted Michael come.

Michael got to the destination exceedingly early. He grabbed a Frank at the Orange Julius. He then waited in the lobby of the hotel, nervously watching the people ~~coming~~ going in and out.

Finally, Misha took him up the elevator. As the door closed, ~~they lifted through the floors,~~ Misha explained to him that everyone was already upstairs. As the door opened to the room, Michael was introduced to four guys who were stranger than Misha. They poured Michael a big glass of wine, and that was the last thing Michael remembered of the evening.

He woke up with a hangover at someone's place in New Jersey. It was not an apartment, but Carl's family home, one of the guys at the party. How was he going to get home? He was somewhere in rural New Jersey. He had school on Monday, and Carl had another man in the room. Carl said it was his brother who was mentally challenged. Carl asked Michael to have sex with him, but his brother must watch. He always watched.

"I just want to go home," said Michael, looking for the exit.

Carl told him he could leave after they did this. All Michael could see from the corner of his eye was Carl's brother staring at them, smiling. Carl did all the action and Michael felt extremely sick at this idea. Carl's brother loved it and clapped his hands. As Michael was leaving, Carl's brother kept smiling telling Michael how great he was, patting him on the back.

Carl gave Michael money to take the bus home and for some food. Michael arrived in the city and could not go home. Carl did say that Andy and Frances were calling Misha's home, asking if they knew where Michael was. They must have gotten Misha's number from his desk. Not knowing what to do; Michael called home. His father asked him to come home, telling him that everything ~~will~~ would be all right.

Michael went home. He was lectured for a while, ~~but~~ and Michael did not blow it off. He knew how much he meant to his parents. His sister came into his room, where Michael was sitting silently. With no compassion she asked him if he was a homosexual. Michael did not answer.

Michael's older cousin Donald, a doctor, was extremely respected by Francis and Andy. When Michael came out of the room, Donald was in the kitchen. His disappointment towards Michael and his actions was clear.

Michael could not sleep, so at about 2 am he hopped out the window of his bedroom and took the A Train back to the Village. When Michael got into the city, he realized he had sophomore orientation the next day. He thought it would be nice to see the sunrise in the city, get breakfast, and go to school. Michael did not understand what had happened in the hotel room. "How did I get to New Jersey? Am I a homosexual?" These thoughts bounced around in his head. He remembered his feelings towards Raphael, but the feelings were not sexual; they were emotional. "I guess answering this is part of the journey," thought Michael.

Michael started to walk toward school, but his pace quickened as he had a feeling deep inside of him that something was wrong. He approached the main lobby of the college, where out of the corner of his eye, he thought he saw his father's car.

Michael walked into the lobby, where he saw his father and Donald. Michael made a break for it, sprinting out the side doors of the building. Donald finally caught up with him. He dragged Michael to the ground and started to beat him up. He lifted Michael up and told him he was a disgrace, as he pushed him against the cyclone fence nearby knocking him to the ground. From the ground, Donald picked Michael back up off the street and ripped his shirt open in the process.

Michael went to get [Pull] the shirt back on, and he realized there was a small pool of blood. One of the links on the fence was sticking out. It pierced Michael's back. He went to the main hall to get some medical treatment. He was greeted by Father Cusack, the college's spiritual advisor, telling Michael never to come back to school. He was kicked out.

Donald sat with Michael in his car driving back home. Donald gave Michael medication, Thorazine, which was an experimental drug given to the schizophrenic. Michael was on the drug for one month. It turned him into a zombie. Michael just stared and said nothing for days.

Donald was trying to get Michael admitted into a psychiatric hospital on Long Island to hopefully get shock therapy treatment. Calm heads prevailed echoed by Andy, and instead, they found an excellent physiatrist in Manhattan.

They brought Michael there at 10 o'clock that night. The family went and met with Dr. Smith, who asked all of them to leave after a while.

Dr. Smith then asked Michael, "Do you want to wear different clothes?"

"No, but I like red shirts," Michael responded, unsure of why this question was asked.

Dr. Smith continued, "Are you happy?"

"Up until the last few weeks, I was." Said Michael.

Dr. Smith smiled; he told Andy he ~~will~~ would not change or "cure" Michael as Donald thought. Two sessions a week, plus group therapy was the RX. What Dr. Smith said made it all click for Michael.

What he said was simple, "Keep what you do to yourself and enjoy your life. Nothing wrong with that. In today's environment, you cannot advertise who you are."

Michael said "I will not advertise, but I am who I am—a great guy who loves and wants to be loved. Okay, doc?" Dr. Smith smiled.

Somehow, Michael was mysteriously admitted to another private university. He later found out that it was Dr. Rossi and Dr. O'Connor that helped. They had lots of friends teaching at the school. They were also very friendly with the Dean of Admissions.

The Thorazine had a lasting effect. Michael would phase out and just stare. When people would ask him what was wrong, Michael claimed that he was only thinking deeply but he was unable to express what he was feeling at the time.

Michael never cared for Donald but respected him and always remembered him ~~with~~ from the scar on his back. Michael felt that Donald was wrong for what he did, but the lesson he learned was that there were many people like Donald. He needed to avoid them in his life or overcome them, as Dr. Smith suggested.

These men were all Reservoir Men— including Donald, the spiritual advisor of the University, and Carl. Michael realized that the universe ended at the threshold of his front door. His relationship with his family, ~~not Frances and Andy,~~ would never be the same. Michael was now alone.

CHAPTER SEVEN

1967-1968

Michael spent the next three months ~~alone~~ ~~in~~ his parent's house. The Thorazine still had a negative effect on his alertness. Michael listened to lots of music and read every book he could get his hands on. He pursued his interests in Buddhism and Hinduism. Siddhartha along with Mao, James Dean, Bob Dylan, and Alan Ginsberg were his heroes. He burnt incense, which drove Frances crazy. But she did not say anything until he brought two large statues of Buddha and Shiva into his room. Frances was terribly upset. They took up so much room, and she did not want to dust them!

Michael felt a hole inside himself, bleeding. Loneliness and separation from who he once was. It all ate away at him. The pain hurt so badly. As much as he hoped for someone to be next to him, there was no one to give him comfort.

Michael was losing weight; he was 6 foot 2 inches tall but clocked in at 156 pounds. He worked out every day. His relationship with his parents was distant. Frances would peer into his room and then shake her head and smile. Christmas came and went. On New Year's Day, Michael convulsed; he could not stop shaking. His parents rushed him to the hospital.

The doctors ran a lot of tests over the next three days. Results of the tests were inconclusive. Doctors put him on medicine to prevent or temper the convulsions. Michael did not take the medicine or any other medicine again; he was tired of people and pills taking his consciousness and his "self" away. He wanted to see the world more clearly.

Spring semester approached, and Michael started his new college The campus was large with a lot of different towering buildings. He had a preplanned academic program by Donald and his father. He studied Science but only one literature class.

The campus was saturated with anti-war and social justice programs and propaganda. Michael's favorite class was literature. Dr. West's reading list went from the Russian to the French and the English. He read

"Crime and Punishment," "Madame Bovary," and "Women in Love." She spoke about how Literature not only reflected a society, but more importantly how it holds the key to understanding ourselves. Michael followed her around at the end of the class like a puppy, as if she carried the tabernacle of enlightenment.

Michael would sit in the quad by himself and smoke a lot. The girls would always check him out on the bench, but this mostly went unnoticed by Michael. He was very conscious of the scar on his lip and would always put a finger over his lip. The smoke from his cigarette would be a veil to hide the scar. Most importantly, the cigarette itself was his lance to protect anyone from getting too close to him or the scar. Michael would fantasize that he was scarred in a duel to the death.

Beverly and Tony, two classmates from Dr. West's class, sat on his bench in the quad without invitation. Both complimented Michael's intelligence. They said he was extremely articulate with constructive interpretations in literature class. Beverly was truly a textbook hippie. She often wore a pioneer dress, long blonde hair, no shoes, and had very black feet. Tony was very smart but gruff with a big build, which did not match his personality. Michael confided in Tony that he was not doing too well in his classes apart from Literature.

Tony looked at Michael's class schedule and said, "You need to escape towards intellectual freedom. Next semester you should take Intellectual Thought of the 18th Century, 20th Century European History, and Dr. West is giving a figure class on William Faulkner. I hear it is the best. Dr. Earl is giving a class on Existentialism, and we will all be together. You must also join SNCC."

Tony was talking about a group whose initials meant the Student Non-violent Coordinating Committee. Michael joined, and Beverly brought him to the entrance of the Manhattan bridge. They just sat in the road with 200 other students. Stopping traffic to the city, protesting the war. Beverly took him to every demonstration in the city.

Michael and Beverley were like the youthful Rosenbergs. Ethel Rosenberg was a hero to Michael, she stood by her truth even in the face of death at her execution. One day, Beverly asked him why he was against the war.

"I don't want to die," said Michael.

Beverly answered, "Satisfactory answer but not quite."

Michael was placed on academic probation for the Spring semester, but he enrolled in all the classes that Tony recommended for the Fall. Michael made many friends, even though he was a bit stiff and shy. It turned out lots of his classmates were also looking for answers.

Michael knew his quest was different. When he spoke in class, he commanded attention and respect. He always made correlations between the novels he was reading and himself, which helped him find a little more of his soul. Michael aced this semester, all A's.

Even in the snow, Michael sat on the bench in the quad. His thoughts wandered to the Reservoir Men and how lonely and desperate they were. They were looking to be accepted by anyone, but that acceptance was not real. They only had moments to retreat from their wife, girlfriend, or mother who were waiting to recapture them into their unfulfilled lives. Michael was not skeptical; he believed in their potential freedom.

Michael was going to summer school to catch up on his credits and make up the lost semester. On a ridiculously scorching summer day, he noticed a hunched over man carrying on like a wild animal, talking to a group of people. This gentleman noticed Michael staring. He came over to his bench with another man and introduced himself as Dean Brown, head of the Business school. Dean Brown introduced the other man as his brother, who said nothing while standing near the bench. Dean Brown invited Michael to visit his office and have a cup of coffee. Tony and Beverly later told Michael that he was one of three powerful men on campus. Michael thought he should and planned to visit him.

Michael and Beverly opened the door to Beverly's apartment sweaty and exhausted after ten hours of demonstrating at the Army Induction Center, being pushed around by the police, spit on by observers, but loved by their fellow protestors.

Michael took a shower, and Beverly looked on waiting for the invitation. Instead, she warmed up the fondu and cut the bread. She opened a bottle of wine. Michael, not a big drinker, sipped the wine and watched the oil bubble while Beverly took her turn in the shower. At this point she knew Michael would not invite himself into the shower.

They sat and fondued. Laughing at the mishaps of the day and all their adventures,

68

Michael drank a lot and Beverly finally got him into the bedroom. She started to undress and then began to undress Michael. Suddenly, they were both naked wrapped in each other's bodies. Michael could not get over how soft Beverly's skin was. He was enjoying moving his hands up and down her body.

Suddenly, Michael left the bed, mumbling to himself. Beverly called him back.

He turned to her and said, "I cannot. It is not right. This is not who I am. I am not a Reservoir Man."

"What is that?" asked Beverly.

Michael turned and said, "Loneliness, despair, a hunger never satisfied. I am setting you up to be hurt. I do not want to hurt you. You are a great person with so much to offer. I want to be your friend, a great friend."

They both laughed, Michael stayed the night, both holding each other. That was the last time Michael saw Beverly because like a magical princess, she just disappeared.

Michael was returning a book to the library and passing the Speech Department offices. He noticed a man standing in the doorway of the

Department. It was Dr. O'Connor from St. Paul's University. He wondered why he was here. He called out to him, quickly going over to him. Dr. O'Connor told Michael how happy he was that Michael was settling into academic life. Michael now had the opportunity to thank him for helping him get into the college as quick as he did. He told Dr. O'Connor to also thank Dr. Rossi as well. Dr. O'Connor excused himself, as he was late for a meeting with a friend.

As he was leaving, a gentleman came out of the offices. Dr. O'Connor introduced Dr. Seller, the chairperson of the Speech Department, to Michael. Standing alone with Dr. Seller, he told Michael he should be an actor because the way he used his arms while talking was dynamic.

Michael said, "Well, I am Italian."

"No, no!" Dr. Seller said, "You do the same type of gestures as John Kennedy."

"Got to go," said Michael.

"I'll walk with you. Where are you going?" said Dr. Seller.

"Home," said Michael.

"Where is that?"

"East New York near City Line," Michael said, trying to walk away.

"I'll drive you part of the way to a closer train station, that's a long trip on the train!" said Dr. Seller with a smile.

As Dr. Seller and Michael approached his destination, Michael was ready to get out. Michael thanked him as he began opening the door. Dr. Seller asked him if he liked anal play. Michael looked at him, not knowing what he meant. Dr. Seller was getting a little nervous and repeated it.

"You know, right?" Michael just shrugged his shoulders and shook his head. "What do you mean? You do not know what I am talking about?" said Dr. Seller in a loud voice. "Your anus!" People outside the car heard him and were peering in at him.

Michael said, "No, I do not understand. I am sorry."

Dr. Seller said, "You better catch your train." He was suddenly cold toward him and looking to drive away.

Michael shut the door as fast as he could. Michael was confused. When he got home, he looked up "anus" in the dictionary. "No way! I might have not learned these words yet; but I know I would never do that. Dr. Seller was a speech teacher; thank God I already took Speech."

Michael spent most of his time at home in his room. He was sad to lose Beverly. No one knew where she went. Frances came into Michael's room.

"Do you remember the Ryan brothers from St. Rita's?" she asked.

"I remember Billy. He was in my grade."

Frances said they were both dead, killed in Vietnam. Mrs. Ryan was attempting to get most of their classmates from grade school and high school to go to the airport and be with the family when they take their bodies off the plane. Without hesitation, Michael agreed to go.

That day, only a hand full of classmates showed up. Michael did not understand why more people did not come. They were afraid of their own reality. Mrs. Ryan just cried and cried. Michael went up and told her how sorry he was. Michael touched the caskets and walked away.

Michael's last year at college was approaching. Dr. West suggested he study comparative literature for his master's and gave him three universities to apply to.

He was taking figure class in the works of Thomas Mann with the head of the German Department. Dr. Bernan invited Michael to his apartment in the city to discuss his academic plans. Somehow Dr. Bernan got Michael into his bedroom. He pushed Michael on the bed, breathing very heavily and smelling of cigarettes and liquor. Michael pushed him away, got up, smiled, thanked him, and left. Well, there goes Thomas Mann. Michael was hungry for the education and the knowledge these people could give to him. He desperately wanted to learn. The problem was that they desperately wanted something else.

Michael talked to Dean Brown at least twice a week. He slowly realized that Dean Brown's brother was really his boyfriend. Michael played along with him because it was Dean Brown's illusion, so he accepted it. Why intrude on his space?

Michael was sitting on his bench when, surprisingly, Dean Brown came out of the Business Building, walked up to him, and said, "Next Friday night, come to school clean and dressed. I have a surprise. Meet me and my brother at the entrance to the campus at seven. Our car will be parked outside of the campus. Look for us, and we will go into the city for a great dinner."

Michael was looking forward to the evening. He liked Dean Brown, and Dean Brown cared for Michael and showed interest in his wellbeing. Approaching the main entrance gate of the college, Michael spotted Dean Brown's car. Michael was well dressed and ~~very~~ ready for a wonderful time.

Michael stuck his head in the passenger side window and spotted a third party in the back of the car. Dean Brown and his brother, sitting in the front of the car, introduced Michael to their friend, Don. Michael hopped into the car, sitting next to Don. Dean Brown made an announcement that they had reservations at the Gay Vienna in Germantown Manhattan. Michael was taken aback, imagining a bunch of Homosexual Viennese dancing slowly to Lieberstraum. In fact, the restaurant was a top NYC eatery, which Dean Brown pointed out a few times. When they got to the restaurant, Michael was impressed. There were men playing violins and the smell of great food but no dancing Austrians.

At the table, Dean Brown told Michael that Don was head of Graduate Admissions to one of the three universities offering comparative literature. Michael was excited that he was with the man who could really advise and guide him. This man could affect his getting into the right university. Michael and Don had great conversations and really hit it off.

The evening ending, they all piled in Dean Brown's car and drove off. They stopped at Don's home on Sutton Place. Don got out of the car, said goodnight, and approached the front door. Dean Brown did not move the car.

Michael said, "My train is only a few blocks away."

Dean Brown firmly said, "Buddy, you get out here. Get out and go upstairs with Don."

Michael froze but understood. He accompanied Don to his apartment. Don made a drink, sat on the couch, and spread his legs. Michael bent over to service him, hoping it would be over soon. Don pushed Michael away and finished Michael off. Michael got up and adjusted himself. Don reached into his pocket and gave him one hundred dollars for a cab to Brooklyn. Michael, keeping his dignity, took the money, said good evening, and jumped into the elevator.

Michael grabbed a cab. In the cab, he thought for the first time about how people viewed him. They viewed him as an object, discounting his intellect. He felt an intellectual void inside himself, a pain, a yearning to be free. He did not want to be the object of someone's pleasure or the object of his own. He wanted the freedom to accept himself and care for those around him. To say, "I am at peace being a homosexual, a young intellectual."

This peace was not with him in the back of the cab. He only felt badly about himself now. He realized this might be his station in life. In his anger, he so wanted to feel not the experience of love, but the minute of getting off. Don too was a Reservoir Man, an image that haunted him. Michael abandoned his hope to study Comparative Literature, never wanting to see Dean Brown again.

The next six months, Michael obsessively sought out anonymous sex. For Michael, this was the "score," the embrace of the Reservoir Men. This was the guy coming toward you that you never knew, and you still never knew him when he finished and walked away. Michael thought he might be chained to this fucking life. He obsessively kept the score, going day after day. He learned not to care but just to finish the objective and go, distancing himself from the path and the truth and his freedom.

CHAPTER EIGHT

1968-1969

Michael had now become, after these last six months, a little more world weary and worse for the wear. Sitting on his bench, entering his last year at college. Michael still had not found his soul or his truth. His emphasis on sex was unfulfilling and empty. He wandered in the shadowy corners, the lightless streets, leading to a dead end and the darkness of an empty truck. Loneliness had become a fixture of Michael's being. He longed for a few hours to be with Carol, Claire, or Raphael.

One day, while sitting on the bench, Michael heard in the distance Otis Reading's "The Dock of The Bay" playing on a portable radio. The music came closer and closer and then quickly turned to the Four Tops' "Reach Out (I'll be There)."

Picking up his head, Michael saw this extremely attractive ethnic guy standing right above him. Michael said 'hello,' and the young man answered.

"My name is Nick. Do you dance?"

Michael said, "Sort of, but I do not have much of a chance to go dancing."

"You want to go tonight?" Nick asked with a smile, and he started to sing "Baby I Need Your Loving" by the Four Tops.

Michael became a little concerned about the message of the song, so he suggested that they might talk over coffee before they venture out dancing. Michael decided to cut his next two classes and have coffee.

They spent hours talking about their lives. Nick was older than Michael by nine years. Nick said he had to prepare for graduation as did Michael. He was in the school for Education and would be graduating that year.

He was first generation Greek from Cyprus and spoke fluent Greek. His family lived in Harlem on 137th Street off Broadway. He had siblings, a brother and sister. Michael was taken by him. He made him laugh and feel amazingly comfortable.

Nick invited Michael to dinner Saturday night. His mother would make Doimadakia, Humus, Tzataki and Moussaka. Michael agreed to go.

Nick's parents were great. His mother was shy, his father a little less. They spoke with a broken accent, which Michael loved. They had a great dinner and talked a lot. Michael learned a lot about Cyprus.

Nick said after dinner, "Dancing, right?"

Michael and Nick left to go dancing. They got on the train to downtown. Nick said they were going to a homosexual club; Michael got a little uncomfortable.

Nick said, "You are a homosexual." This was a major moment in Michael's life even though he never admitted it to someone.

Michael found the courage and said, "Sure." They got to the club.

Nick said, "Look, Michael, do not move your arms too much. The motion is in the legs and hips. Slightly use your hands and arms."

Michael understood this because of his love for music, and he felt the beat. He danced all night and never stopped. Walking to the train, Nick asked Michael to sleep at his house that night. Michael politely declined.

He ~~Michael~~ spent the next few months pushing away Nick's romantic advances and worrying about the war in Vietnam. Nick took Michael to what felt like every club in NYC. Nick even convinced ~~Michael~~ him to go to a Cuban Club in Harlem.

"They love gay guys," he said.

After the first dance they were asked to leave. Michael admired Nick's zest for people and life. Frances and Andy liked Nick but were cautious. Especially when Michael started sleeping in Harlem. They trusted their son; nothing from the past clouded their judgment. Andy was still hoping Michael's bride would walk through the door. Frances did not care, as long as her son was happy, and he lived his life in privacy.

Nick and Michael talked a lot about the draft and how soon they would be drafted after graduation. Nick said he was going to Europe for six months right after graduation, spending some time with his family in Cyprus.

He asked Michael to go with him, telling him that, "You can get a student deferment for seven to eight months while independently studying in a foreign country."

Michael got excited, not because of the deferment. He realized that this was what the British Victorians gave their male children. When they graduated, they sent them to the continent for an extended time. The deferment was more attractive to Andy than having a Victorian son. Frances was very uneasy about this venture.

Michael told his father, "Do not buy me a car for graduation. Send me to Europe."

Andy agreed but the deal was that Michael had to use his graduation money as well. Michael got his deferment and bought his ticket to Amsterdam on Lufthansa Airlines. Nick's brother worked for TransCaribbean Airlines, he gave Nick free plane trips through Europe and Cyprus. Michael bought a First Class Eurail pass for three months. This permitted him to go first-class from city to city in Europe with no reservations, nor restrictions, for as many trips as he wanted. They both were skipping graduation.

Though Andy and Frances felt bad not seeing their son graduate, they knew this adventure was important. His parents went to the airport with him, watched him go through customs,

82

and stood looking down at him entering his gate.
He promised to write every day and to light candles
in every church he visited for the family. Michael
was just twenty years old but felt as if he had
already lived a lifetime.

This was Michael's first flight. He stared out
the window into total darkness, like the void that
used to be in his soul. The darkness was intense.
Seeing the sun rise toward the end of the flight was
a burst of radiance and safety welcoming him to a
new home.

Landing in Amsterdam was extraordinary.
He walked off the plane not knowing what anyone
was saying. As time went on, Michael felt that he
started to understand their language, not knowing
a word of Dutch. From the airport he went directly
to the Bed and Breakfast he pre-booked for a few
days before departing to meet Nick.

At the house/hotel, a nice woman, very
physically broad, greeted him and brought him
upstairs to his room. She told Michael where and
when breakfast was served. Michael took a nap,
woke up, and it was still light outside. He checked
his watch, and it was 10 pm. He went outside, and
he saw the architecture in greater detail for the
first time. It was incredible.

The Dutch people seemed at ease and happy. He sat on a bench at one of the canals and watched the people. His understanding was beginning to develop. He sensed the Dutch people had fears, desires, and compassion. Most of all, Michael felt that they all somehow harnessed their own personal freedom.

Michael left Amsterdam to meet Nick in Paris. Nick met Michael at the train station, where ~~they could book a hotel cheaply. Nick always arrived in the city before Michael. Nick flew from city to city.~~

Michael fell in love with Paris from the moment he stood on the Boulevard Saint-Germain. The architecture, the smell, and the comfortableness of the people engulfed his senses.

Michael, as promised, lit a candle in all churches they visited for Andy and Frances. He also sent a postcard to his parents every day from all the cities. Nick respected Michael and gave him his space in all the churches they visited. Nick himself was not big on religion, but he watched Michael light each candle and often joined him on the quest.

The hours he would spend in a church were endless. Michael got much more from this environment than he could express. Meanwhile, Nick sat in the back of the church or went outside to smoke.

Michael told Nick, "Look at the beauty. Look at how these people who built these churches loved whatever God represented to them."

The serenity, the culture, these people had something that Michael wanted to know and have. He could feel it all around him, in every hand-crafted loving detail. Michael watched two young men walk hand and hand, not signaling a relationship but friendship instead. It was okay here. Travelling from France to Germany, Austria, and Switzerland, all roads led to Italy. Michael became intoxicated with the antiquity and the beauty of the countries.

On their last night in Rome, Michael decided to take a walk alone. He went out of the lobby and saw people walking rapidly in one direction. He followed them to Roma Termini, the largest train station in Rome. It was across the plaza from the ancient Roman Baths, the Diocletian.

There was a huge stage with lots of lights. Michael had no idea what was to come. Suddenly a woman slowly walked on stage looking incredibly sexy. Her first song was ~~so~~ very emotional. A woman behind Michael said she was Mina and began to translate her songs for Michael's benefit. Mina sung about lovers who she longed for but could not take back, repeating "no" numerous times. She sang so strongly, knowing the joy and disappointment of love. What a night! Piaf has a companion; Michael's love for Mina's music was enormous—Mina and Piaf, what a duo!

Preparing for their trip to Cyprus, Michael was to take the train to Brindisi. He would then board a boat to Patras, Greece. The boat ride was eighteen hours to Patras. He would then take a bus to Athens. Nick was to meet him at the Hotel Stanley. Nick planned Michael's trip hour to hour; he was concerned about Michael's safety. Michael arrived in Brindisi hours before boarding.

There were numerous labor strikes in the town by the communist party. Michael sat and watched. He took a break to get bread, provolone, and salami, impressed by the passion of the men. He had no idea why they were striking, but it must be important.

While eating his bread and salami, he met a German couple that spoke English. He shared his food and asked why they were striking.

The couple laughed and said, "They do this every day around lunch time."

They ~~cautioned~~ advised Michael to buy his ticket since they missed the boat twice both days, ~~they had no more seats.~~ The seats were all sold. Michael booked a shared cabin so he would not have to sleep on the deck in airplane seats. Those seats were shaped like they were on an airplane, and they were just as uncomfortable. Ready to go. They boarded, letting the cars go on first, then the passengers. The German couple had deck seats, ~~but~~ and Michael stayed with them before making it to his cabin.

The couple made a friend while waiting to board. His name was Maritzo. He was a very classy, good looking, older person who was from Rhodes and owned a textile mill.

He asked Michael, "Is this your first trip to Europe?"

Michael responded blankly, "Does it show?"

"You look so sad. Do you smile?" asked Maritzo. Michael gave him a broad smile, and the Greek was satisfied.

Michael went to his cabin to find it was filled with six Greek boys who were studying in Italy. Michael was tall, 6 foot 2, which was extraordinary for these guys who were barely 5 feet 4 inches. They wanted to be Michael's friend and showed him photos of their family and girlfriends. Michael was polite and shared their life for two hours.

Michael excused himself and went up to the deck to get something to eat. He saw the German couple, and they were still with Maritzo. Michael joined them. In the evening, Maritzo asked Michael to join him driving to Athens and not to take the bus, which was extremely uncomfortable. Michael declined, but the German couple urged Michael to go with Maritzo, as he had an MG. Michael did not care about the man's car.

The German couple insisted, "You'll have a wonderful time."

Michael did not answer. He did not want another sexual situation, especially in a foreign country. Michael went back to his cabin, where the six Greek guys were asleep. Michael did not sleep well. He got up early and went to the main deck. He noticed everyone was asleep in their seats. He saw an empty bench and made himself comfortable. He noticed Maritzo smoking towards the middle of the boat.

He said to himself, "Shit, it cannot be worse than all those other situations."

He walked to Maritzo and asked, "Where do I join you?"

Maritzo ruffled his hair and said warmly, "You'll make a great driving companion."

The smoke from Maritzo's cigarette floated into the blackness of the night, the void beyond the boat, beyond the sea. Michael turned away from it, toward the orange glow of the lights on the deck, wishing he were already in Athens.

~~After a pause "Let's go," said Michael~~ with ~~vigor.~~ After a pause, Michael said with vigor, "Let's go."

They were ready to depart. Michael went to the car deck. He saw Maritzo standing next to a small red two-seater sports car. Michael approached the car, put his luggage in the back, and said, "Ready." Maritzo put his arms around Michael.

"We are going to have a wonderful time; we have two stops before Athens. I am going to take you a bit out of the way for you to see two great sites."

As they left the ship at Patras, Michael saw the German couple waving toward him. "Well, here goes," thought Michael, his thoughts of Maritzo turning from sexual predator to lunatic who might kill him. His anxiety grew rapidly.

Michael hugged the door, almost hanging out. Maritzo had the radio on, somber and sad Greek songs. Michael felt the emotion in the singer's voice and almost understood what he was singing. With the breeze blowing in Michael's hair, he slowly fell asleep.

Michael woke up after an hour or so and saw a jacket on him, like a blanket. Maritzo had taken his jacket off and laid it on Michael. Michael grabbed it and smiled at Maritzo, and they began to talk. He did not understand how Maritzo was able to talk with all the wind while they were driving, more so how he was able to understand him. He told Michael that the Greek people are special. They understand the pain of living but easily turn it into hope and determination. They love the joy of just being alive.

At Delphi, Maritzo said he knew a small hotel with great food. Michael turned away from him and rolled his eyes.

"That means they have beds," thought Michael.

He wondered why they could not just drive through to Athens. They checked into the lovely hotel. Michael was relieved to find he had his own room. After he cleaned up, he went downstairs to find Maritzo. Maritzo was outside looking at the mountains.

"We are at the center of the world; Zeus took two eagles; one flew to the East the other to the West, and they met in Delphi. Michael, now you are free to live the choices you want. You are in Delphi," said Maritzo with a warm smile. There were a few tables facing the mountains. Maritzo ordered Retsina for them to drink.

meantime

"We will order food soon, but sit here and watch the mountains," he instructed.

They sat quietly for about an hour when suddenly the sun began to set. A golden burst of light came over the mountains. It was one of the most inspirational sights Michael ever saw in his entire life. When it became dark, lights appeared everywhere hanging from trees over the hotel building. It was truly magical.

Maritzo told him, "The Oracles at Delphi are ready to tell us the future."

They laughed and ordered dinner. A Greek salad, red caviar, and humus. The entree, Moussaka, and grilled shrimp. Dessert was custard and honey with Phyllo. Michael could not stop thanking Maritzo. No one ever gave and shared with Michael like this. Maritzo and Michael laid on the grass looking at a beautiful night sky. Maritzo told Michael he must never lose hope.

He said to Michael, "Hope brings you peace of mind. Then you make the decision to move ahead. You must always love, not another person, though that is important, but all persons. That is humanity. That is your job." Michael fell asleep on his shoulder.

Michael awoke in his own bed. He got ready and met Maritzo in the courtyard having breakfast. Lots of fruit, olives, and cheeses. After coffee, they got in the car. The ride was longer than yesterday. They finally got to their destination, another small hotel, but Maritzo took Michael in the back of the hotel.

There was a tree with gigantic roots around the trunk. Maritzo ordered a bottle of Retsina, and they sat under the olive tree. It was one of the oldest trees in Greece.

Maritzo told Michael, "The olive tree brings peace and friendship. I brought you here to bond our friendship. And Michael, you will find peace. It will come to you by fate, not by looking for it."

Michael told Maritzo they could sleep together tonight. Maritzo pulled a small white flower from the grass and put it in Michael's hand, and he put his finger to Michael's lips, "Zeus did not make that choice for us at Delphi. We will forever be loving friends."

The drive to Athens the next morning was quick. Michael did not say a word, but he was concerned about Nick, who had been waiting two days for him, hoping he did not file a missing person's report. Michael could not imagine Nick standing there for the entire two days! As they approached the Hotel Stanley, Michael saw Nick standing outside, hysterical. Maritzo knew of Nick through his conversations with Michael. Maritzo told them he was leaving tomorrow night for Rhodes. He would like to take them out tonight and lunch tomorrow.

That evening they went into the hills around Athens. He took them to a country restaurant with lights, tables outside, and traditional Greek music. They had a wonderful time. They ate Souvlaki and large Greek salads.

As they walked to the car, Michael stopped Maritzo and said, "I am going to miss you."

"I will always be near you. Remember our experience, and if you drink Retsina, pour a glass for me at the table," said Maritzo.

The next day he took them for an early lunch at King Constantine's yacht club. Very elegant and special. They said their goodbyes to Maritzo, and Michael and Nick took a cab back to the hotel. Nick asked him if he slept with Martizo.

"No," Michael replied.

"Why?" said Nick.

"He gave me a path instead." Michael walked away from Nick.

Every Christmas, Michael got a beautiful card from Maritzo. It was always mailed to his parents' house, the only address he had. He got a card for over twenty years. Then, one year, it stopped. Maritzo never put a return address on the envelope. Michael thought that was for the better.

Everything that was to be said was said. Michael loved him.

CHAPTER NINE

1969-1970

Michael was feeling empty and a little lost after his departure from Greece.

Nick did not stop insisting, "You slept with him, right?"

Michael firmly said, "No, and stop asking me. It is all inside me. It is a feeling I do not understand. I feel it in the pit of my stomach. There is a lot for me to figure out."

Nick was getting a little hot under his collar, "You are in love with this guy, and you are telling me you did not sleep with him being on a two-day journey through Greece? Bull."

"I love him but not like you think." Nick was very confused, "Nick, let us make a deal not to talk about this ever again. This feeling is special in me. I want to hold on to it. I am happy."

"Deal! But could you tell me what happened when you guys took two days to get to Athens when it is only a six-hour drive?" asked Nick.

"Nothing. We just drove," Michael gave Nick a kiss on his cheek and walked away.

Nick and Michael were standing in Athen's airport looking for their flight to Cyprus. The plane was not in the terminal. They had to walk on the field past numerous planes when they finally saw a little 20-seater plane. The plane took off, barely. It took them one hour and thirty-five minutes to land in Nicosia, the capital of Cyprus. Nicosia was diversified with both Greeks and Turks; it was jointly governed by both. Nick's family did not meet them at the airport.

Nicosia was hot and incredibly old. Lots of Greek orthodox priests in their multitude of layers of dark clothes walked the streets. The country was war torn between the Greeks and the Turks, and you could sense the tension as you were walking through the streets. They were Americans. Michael was tall and stood out, and everyone looked at him because of his height.

They grabbed a bus to Larnaca, a Greek part of the country, where Nick's family lived. The bus was hot and humid. They bumped their way to Larnaca. Arriving in Larnaca, Michael was surprised how peaceful the city felt. It looked like the postcards from California beaches with lots of palm trees. The Mediterranean was inviting and calm.

Michael again noticed that no one from Nick's family met them at the bus station, and they had to walk to his family's house. They were sweating and breathing heavily when they finally reached their destination. The temperature was 112 degrees.

Nick's family on his mother's side lived very poorly, but they greeted them with such joy. Michael and Nick put their luggage down in their bedroom, which was smaller than the smallest American bedroom. They were fed, and the food was bountiful and delicious. They slept in the same room with four of the young men in the family. The house was hot, but no one cared.

Michael relished the family. They had so much love toward him and Nick. Everyone smoked, and the whole house looked like a London fog. Michael did not sleep the first night because he had so much fun with the guys. No one spoke English, but their hand gestures passed the test. Nick whispered to Michael that in a few days, they were going to stay with his father's family. It would be more comfortable.

"I like it here!" said Michael.

The young men took Michael out before they left for Nick's other relatives. Michael had ouzo for the first time, and it hit him badly. Michael and the guys all sat in the water at the beach and laughed.

Michael bonded with the guys without talking their language. The feeling of companionship, the bond between them, grew stronger as the days past. ~~past.~~ Michael thought of ~~passed~~ soldiers at war; this must be the same bond. He left that morning, looking back at them as they walked from the house.

Michael said to Nick, "Even though they are poor, it does not matter. They love life. They find their happiness every day."

They were now standing on an elaborate porch of a beautiful home. Nick's other family members were there, and they all politely kissed and hugged Nick as Michael stood in the background. The house keepers came out with fresh fruit and cheese. They sat and talked. The mother and father were genuinely nice. They had two children named Nikos and Nikki. Michael looked puzzled.

"Nikos and Nikki?" said Michael. "But then, you have Nick too. This must be an immensely popular name in the family?" Michael was told the father was head of the Communist party in Cyprus. It was all adding up.

Michael liked his room, which he did not have to share with Nick. The house cleaner came in with additional sheets and pillows. He could only think, "Wow, we are here for three weeks."

Nikki and Nikos where about two years apart. Nikki was beautiful, and Nikos was very handsome. Nikki was the promotional face of Cyprus; her face was on all the publications for tourism. Nikos was going to school in Athens, studying to be a lawyer. The father was close with the President of Cyprus, the Archbishop Makarios. The father was also the head of import and export for Cyprus. They were rich but did not play it up. They made Michael feel amazingly comfortable. The family loved Nick.

Michael never experienced comfort like he did in Cyprus. Nick's family took him all over the island, from the mountains to an exclusive beach resort in Famagusta. He became close to both Nikki and Nicos.

Nikki looked after Michael with gentle caring. She called him Michail Mou, which meant "My Michael." It was one of the many times he felt the tenderness of a woman. Her touch was soft, and she understood him. It was genuinely great.

Her brother Nico developed a strong relationship with Michael, and they talked and drank lots of Turkish Coffee. They talked about the things that young people did at this time, about God, love, war, and peace. ~~Michael loved Turkish Coffee.~~ Nikki and her mother would tell fortunes with the coffee cup. They turned the cup upside down on its saucer, and the imprint from the grounds would tell a story.

Michael spent a few nights talking to their father, who explained the importance of Communism in underdeveloped nations, like Cyprus, and how the poor are protected. The State must provide for all their people. Michael understood it in his own way.

Time to leave Cyprus. Michael went over to the other family to say goodbye. They had food and gifts waiting for him.

They told him in Greek, "You are a good man, strong and loving. We will never forget you and those drunken nights."

Michael smiled, thanked them, and went up to each one and kissed them on both cheeks as they reciprocated. He went back to Nikki and Nicos, and to his surprise, Nicos was getting his father's car to take them to the Airport in Nicosia.

Michael thought, "I hit this one out of the park. They are driving me to the airport!"

They got to the airport and, while getting ready to board the plane, Nikki said to Michael, "Michail Mou, I will come to America in two months to visit my aunts in Virginia."

Michael was happy knowing she will meet his family. Nicos came to Michael and kissed him on both cheeks. Michael thought with a smile, "I waited three weeks for that."

Michael kissed Nicos back on both cheeks. Their flight left for Athens.

Nick was able to help get Michael a cheap flight to Madrid from Athens. It would have taken Michael four days to go from Athens to Madrid by Eurail. In Madrid, they had a great bed and breakfast right off the Prado. The Spaniard's stayed up late and had dinner late. The noise outside their window was loud. Michael enjoyed going to the Prado, just looking at people.

The next morning at breakfast, they shared a table with two Indian girls from Durban, South Africa. Their names were Nyra and Hana, and they were dressed ethnically. Michael loved it. He learned a lot about apartheid and how oppressive their life was. Michael could not understand how this could be happening in the free world today.

Michael gave the girls special attention. Nick was going to Segovia to see a friend. The girls came, got ~~a great chance~~ to see the Roman Aqueduct, and had a lot of fun. Back in Madrid, they spent hours in the Prado Museum. Then Nyra and Hana had to leave. They said they were going to Lisbon. Michael made plans to meet up with them in Lisbon. He and Nick took them to the airport and saw them off.

Michael and Nick decided to take a cab back to the hotel. Michael ran to the first cab he saw and jumped in. One of the many military men came up to the cab and told Michael to get out.

Michael asked why and said, "You must be crazy taking me out of the cab."

The military man understood English and arrested Michael. He put him in a police car and drove to the police station. Nick was right behind in a cab. Michael was put in a jail, in a cell facing an empty table with two chairs and a rifle leaning on one of the chairs. The guard came to the cell and asked him questions in Spanish, but Michael did not understand him.

Nick came into the room. He looked at Michael and said, "You cannot fool around with these people."

Franco had been in power for a long time and discipline was the order. Michael still did not know what he did. Nick, being fluent in Spanish, talked and talked to the superior. It seemed not to help.

He left the room and Nick came over to Michael to explain what he did, "You have to que and then take your cab, not just run, and get the first one. And then you told the police officer he was crazy too. Now you are arrested. Start praying."

An hour went by, and a superior military man came in and spoke to Nick in Spanish. The guard picked up his gun, and Michael thought that were going to kill him for getting in the wrong cab.

He came over to the cell, opened it, and Nick said, "Let's get out of here, now."

They walked back to the hotel for 3 hours, but Michael felt safe and could not stop thanking Nick. Michael got to the train station, leaving for Lisbon. He was amazed by all the military standing around with rifles on their shoulders. Michael made a promise that he would never forget to que for a taxi again, no matter where he was, even in New York.

As Michael's train pulled into Lisbon, there was Nick, on the platform waiting for him to arrive. They were able to get a room where the girls from South Africa said they were staying, which was not too far from the train station. They checked in and asked the woman at the desk if the girls had also checked in.

She said, "No, sorry."

Michael and Nick went out and walked around and noticed how sad the people were. The military was just as bad in Lisbon as in Madrid. Salizar was the leader for a long time. He was also a fascist like Franco.

Nick's plane left in three days for America. Michael had to wait eight days before his plane left from Amsterdam to New York. Michael had five days to kill before travelling to Amsterdam. Michael decided to stay in Lisbon for a few more days. Nick's departure was emotional, especially on Nick's part. They hugged and hugged. Michael walked him to a cab, as they queued. And Nick left. Michael walked back into the B&B and sat in the dining room by himself.

The woman at the front desk came over and said, "You must go to the beaches. They are beautiful. There is one beach at Estoril, outside of Lisbon. The train goes right to the beach."

The next day, Michael went to the beach. The train went right there, but she failed to tell him it was a long walk to the beach. Michael finally made it. He sat on a bench facing the sea.

Suddenly, this very good-looking tall man sat down, smiling. He introduced himself as Adriano and said he lived in one of those small cottages right on the ocean. He spoke wonderful broken English. He invited Michael for a cup of coffee and a sweet. Michael accepted and they walked along the shore to a small coffee shop. As they walked, people knew Adriano, and the whole coffee house knew him as well.

An older man came over, put his arms around him, and told him, "You are more than good."

They had a polite conversation. Adriano took off his jacket. Michael looked in disbelief. His right arm was a small arm with small fingers.

Adriano said, "I am sorry. I am a Thalidomide baby. Mothers who were pregnant took Thalidomide to prevent nausea."

Michael was aware of this condition. When the theory about the ball hitting Frances' stomach was dispelled, everyone assumed that Frances took Thalidomide and that was what produced Michael's hair lip. That was not the case since the drug was never approved in the USA, only for experimental purposes. But tens of thousands of children in Europe were born like this—some with no limbs at all.

Michael said, "So what? Look at my lip. This is all a burden that makes us accept who we are and stronger."

Adriano asked Michael to come home with him. Michael hesitated and really did not want to go. Adriano looked so disappointed.

He said, "You don't have a friend?"

107

Michael said, "No, it is hard to find someone." Michael continued, "But Adriano, you have a great personality and such a great soul. If you were in America, you would be my top choice. You are the man." Adriano just smiled.

"All the people around here love me," said Adriano. "These people raised me. My mother died a few months after my birth, and my father went back out to sea, never to be seen again. I lived with my aunt and all the town people." Michael smiled.

He thought about how special this guy was. He wanted to be with him. Michael finally made up his mind, saying, "I will stay, Adriano, the whole night."

"Well," said Adriano, "at low tide, I want to show you something magical."

The morning came and what a night. They walked to the shore in the morning. Adriano showed Michael Pedro do Sol, beautiful salt stones. Adriano said they were millions of years old. People come from all over the world to study them. Adriano pulled some from the sea.

"Touch them and remember me," said Adriano.

"How could I forget?" said Michael.

They went back to the cottage and held each other for a while. These last hours with Adriano were serene and genuinely loving. Michael took a cab to the train. When he left, he looked at Adriano and took his handicap arm to say goodbye.

"I will never forget; I only wish I could stay longer," said Michael. "Forever." He thought sadly to himself.

Michael was back in Lisbon and began packing for Amsterdam, then America. He got to the train station five hours before the train left for France. He found a quiet bench, and while sitting comfortably alone, he remembered Adriano. He remembered Adriano's innocent face, the magic of his stories, the tenderness of his touch as Michael held on to the rocks from the sea. Adriano was one of a very few people Michael slept with and remembered fondly, unlike all those anonymous encounters.

Deep in thought, Michael did not notice that a woman sat next to him. She gently pushed Michael's arm. She introduced herself as Maria, asking if Michael was American. She was delighted to hear his answer. Maria was going to France, to a small town over the border. She was travelling second class. Michael was first class.

Boarding the train, Maria sat with Michael in his first-class compartment. No one else was seated. They talked a lot. She was socialist and anxious to overthrow the Salizar government. As the train was preparing to depart, the conductor came into the compartment, looked at the tickets, and told Maria she must return to second class.

Michael, after feeling lonely in his compartment for a short while, walked back to second class to be with Maria. When he found her compartment, his eyes widened to see four other ladies of all sizes and ages in the compartment. Maria introduced them all as her journeywomen, all going to the small town over the French border. Michael went with Maria to the hallway outside of the compartment in second class. The train came to a stop as they pulled into the station.

Michael hung out the window to buy sandwiches for all the ladies from the vendors. While eating, Michael looked out the window and saw the reflection of the train in the moonlight. He saw smoke coming from the engine and realized he was on a coal burning train.

Confused, he looked at Maria, and she responded, "You did not know this was a Rapido train? It makes lots of stops and it is very inexpensive. We will change engines at the Spanish border and go much faster with fewer stops."

Michael nodded and said good night. He told Maria he would see her at the French border. His first-class compartment was still empty. At the first station crossing, a couple came into his compartment, and they were Americans. They were just married. He was a lawyer; she was a teacher. They explained to Michael that they could pull both seats opposing each other together to make a full bed. Michael felt it would be better not to do it.

Michael began falling asleep when suddenly the compartment door opened with the conductor and an older couple. The conductor demanded very aggressively the chairs be put back, so the couple can sit. The lawyer quickly awakened, and out of nowhere, he began to throw punches at the conductor.

The police came on the train from the station. Michael hunched under the confusion and got out of the car. He realized he needed to get away. He needed to get to Maria. As he began walking quickly down the hall to second class, he noticed out the window the couple being dragged off the train and pushed against a wall.

Michael opened Maria's door quickly and emotionally told her the story. He believed the police officers were also looking for him as well. All five women got out of the compartment, they lifted the seats and hid Michael under the seat. After a while, Michael heard the police in their compartment looking for the other American. An hour later, they got Michael to come out, he was sweating a lot. They explained to Michael he must lay low until they get to the Spanish/French border and run to Hendaye in the French section.

Maria told Michael that when they come to the border and depart, the passengers walk up a long ramp going to the border station. When they get to the end of the ramp, they have left Spain. The women will walk all around Michael, so he cannot be seen amongst them.

The Spainards did not check passports. They left it to the French instead. In France, they had to walk down another long ramp just on the opposite side, parallel to where they entered. At the end of the parallel ramp, there were French customs agents.

The women began their journey up the ramp. Michael towered over them, so he had to stay hunched. He saw through two of the women a

112

great sight, the Pyrenees Mountains. Michael picked up his head in amazement, all five women pulled his head back down. They were now out of Spain, and France was easy! Michael was safe. He gave the agents his passport and he was free.

They all got the train to Paris. Michael sat in the second-class car with his saviors, the women who brought him to freedom. A few bottles of wine were opened; the women toasted each other. Maria gave Michael another bottle for the rest of his trip.

Michael made it to Paris. He had to go to another station for his train to Amsterdam. He hopped a cab and got to the train station as quickly as possible, afraid he might be late. Michael ran to his train only to find out he was incredibly early. In arriving in Amsterdam, he decided not to go into town but wait the ten hours at the airport before his plane left. He was incredibly early; He found a bench. The bench was long and plastic, but it was still a bench.

He thought about everything he had experienced. What an exciting time understanding so much about people. The most important thing he learned was to bond with people, whether it was with Maritzo, Adriano, the four Greek guys,

Nikki, or even the German couple. That bond gave friendship a powerful foundation. It embraced compassion, truth, commitment, caring, and sharing. This was Michael's ultimate rite of passage. He had the foundation to understand humanity as well as himself. Michael was now on the path to freedom.

On the way to the departure gate, Michael passed a bookstore. He quickly looked at all the obscure books on display. Suddenly, he saw something unexpected, the Red Book! Mao's Red Book. The book Nikki's father showed him. He bought it.

Sitting on the plane, he would ~~waive~~ wave the book in the air to get the attention of the Stewardess for coffee. While millions of Chinese Communists waved their book in the air while listening to Mao's Speeches, Michael did the same but for coffee.

When having conversations with other passengers, they would ask his name. "I'm Michael," he said, all the while thinking about the others, he had with him too. He had Adriano, Maritzo, Maria, Nicos, Nikki, Mina, and so many more. They were all coming home with him. ✳

CHAPTER TEN

1971-1974

Michael exited the plane and walked down a long ramp to Customs. Customs was in a pit, and above was a viewing gallery. While looking up from the pit, he saw Frances and Andy smiling down at him. It looked as if his mother Frances had her nose pushed against the window. Michael left customs.

The doors opened, and there they were. Michael was so happy to see them both. As they walked towards the parking lot, Andy and Frances had their arms around his waist. What a sight! Michael had suffered a hair lip, broken arm, his harelip appendix, school grades, misdiagnosis, and all his attempts to break free, but they were always there for him.

He loved them so much, but he feared the obstacle of who he was. Michael wondered "How will they feel toward me?" This knowledge could change their great relationship. Michael knew he was making a change in his intellectual awareness by traveling, which opened his mind to other directions in life and seeing other dimensions in the world. But Andy and Frances would always see Michael as a loving son.

His mother Frances made macaroni and sausages. Michael did not even unpack. He dug in as Frances' sauce was the best. He could drink it. She took out at least one hundred postcards sent by Michael. Andy said he so appreciated the post cards as they did not worry about Michael at all, except when there were two weeks with no postcards. The mail carrier knocked on the door one day, with quite a few postcards.

Michael told them he lit a candle in all the churches that he visited. He asked his parents, "Did you feel the power across the ocean?" They laughed but appreciated the gesture. Michael went into his room to get all the gifts he got for them and noticed two big packages. Frances told him that they came for him two weeks ago. had gotten

Michael opened both large packages. He received two large hand-carved African masks made of ebony; they were beautiful. He opened the letter attached to the package. As he read, he realized it was from the South African girls. They had to leave suddenly; their father took ill. They left a message at the hotel, but on the flight home, they realized they had the wrong hotel. Michael knew they were friends. He went out the next day and bought them gifts. He wrote a long letter telling them about Adriano, not everything, just the pieces he wanted to share.

Frances and Andy were showered with gifts from all the countries Michael visited. The next evening, they ordered Chinese. As they were eating, the phone rang, and it was Nick. "He wants me to come over," he told his parents.

Michael decided to be alone for a few days, if not longer. He sat the next few nights on a bench looking out at the ocean. He wondered if he ~~will~~ would ever meet friends here in New York like those in Europe. He longed for the joy they gave him, the security and peace. He had two problems to clear up now, the first being, where does he go with his degree, and the second, what to do about the draft?

He so much wanted to continue with literature. He focused on colleges in California but did not want to leave Frances and Andy. Dealing with the draft was the most important thing because he did not want to die. His deferment would be up in three weeks. Andy did not want him to go. All of Frances' brothers were in the Navy, and one died in World War II. Andy advised his son to play it out, let them see where it ended up. Michael didn't understand playing it out, but his father was generally right, so he waited.

Michael went up to Nick's house and was greeted warmly by his parents. They made dinner, and Nick's brother and sister also joined them. Nick told Michael he had a surprise; he was informed by the draft board that if you took graduate Education classes towards a masters, you could maintain your deferment. Nick showed Michael the paper, and he made a commitment to go back to his undergraduate school and enroll in the graduate program. Michael did what Nick said, and he got the deferment. Andy was right, just let it play out.

In his second semester, Michael got two shocks, the first was that the government eliminated the graduate school deferment, except for science. The second shock was that Nikki was coming to America in a few months, staying with her relatives in Norfolk. Nick told Michael that Nikki wanted to marry him.

"I never even touched her; how could she think that?" asked Michael.

"Maybe she saw more in your eyes than you even knew was there," answered Nick.

Michael looked perplexed, "You're in some other movie, not mine. Not here, and now."

Suddenly, Michael got his draft notice. He had to report to Floyd Bennets Field in Brooklyn. He had two weeks. Andy was looking for a way to save his son.

"You still have that stomach problem?"

"Sure, a little bit," said Michael.

"Before you get drafted, make an appointment with this doctor in the city. Let him check you out."

Michael did as his father said. The doctor pushed here and there around Michael's stomach. He wanted to do an X-ray now.

After the x-ray, he told Michael to wait, saying, "Go get something to eat, and come back in three hours. I should have the results."

Michael returned, and the doctor told him he had an ulcer. "I am going to give you the x-rays, be careful with them," said the doctor. Michael came home and spoke to his father. Andy told him to take them to the induction.

Five o'clock in the morning, ~~at the gates~~ of Floyd Bennent field. ~~Andy drove Michael and~~ told ~~him~~ to call when he was ready. Michael walked to the first barracks and sat in a room filled with young men. At the corner of his eye, he saw a classmate from college, Eugene, so he sat next to him. Michael had a comrade on his journey to the gallows.

They were taken into a room where they needed to strip down to their underwear. They went from barracks to barracks taking all types of medical tests. Some guys were eliminated before they reached the end. But Eugene and Michael made it all the way to the end. Michael tried to give his x-rays to someone, but he wound up carrying them all day.

Finally, Michael saw a doctor, he went over to him and gave him the x-rays. The doctor took him down an empty hallway. Eugene was barely able to say goodbye, telling Michael he would see him soon. Michael sat outside the door for about two hours. He asked if he could call his parents, and he was told 'no.'

120

A high-ranking officer came out and told Michael [him] to go in and sit down. Michael sat with two doctors in front of him and a military man wandering around with his x-rays. The military guy told Michael they did not think he had an ulcer.

One of the doctors persisted, asking him, "Do you, Michael? Do you believe you have an ulcer?"

Michael responded calmly, "If my doctor says so." The military guy took his x-rays and threw them at Michael.

"Take your fucking ulcer out of here. No 4F for you, a 1Y."

Michael understood what they did. A 4F means you can never be drafted, a 1Y means you can still be drafted if the war got bad. It was midnight when Andy [his father] picked him up. Michael and Andy went to the diner to talk. Andy called Frances; they were happy he was staying home. Michael never saw Eugene again. He found out later that Eugene was killed his first month in Vietnam.

Michael questioned the situation with the stomach doctor. It bothered him to have a diagnosis of an ulcer with no follow up

121

appointment or medicine. He believed his father had something to do with the doctor. He wondered if his father was conspiring with the doctor. "Sure," he said, "great for me to not go overseas, but did those other guys have a chance like I did? What about Eugene? His family and his life?"

Michael spoke to Nick a lot about his feelings. Nick told him to forget it and that his father loved him and wanted to see him fulfill his dreams. Michael agreed, but the empty feeling never left him, never! What a horrible cycle of life—you are born, then die for something at 18 you do not understand.

Nikki arrived from Cyprus. Nick and Michael flew down to Norfolk, Virginia to meet her. She was staying with her aunts. For reasons unknown to Michael, they had to stay in a hotel though her aunts had a big house. Nikki and Michael spent a lot of time together. Her aunts were very generous, and everyone had a wonderful time.

Michael and Nick got jobs as case workers with the Department of Welfare. Nikki was coming up to New York in a few weeks, and Michael promised to show her ~~New York~~ the city. Nick knew Michael liked the darker scene, and he warned him not to show Nikki that part of New York.

Nikki was staying with Nick's family. Michael would also occasionally stay there. He Michael took Nikki home to meet his family, and they fell in love with her. Michael's parents were leaving for Mexico and invited Nikki to stay at the house with Michael.

Michael the was shocked that they would suggest this. "They are hoping the magic would will happen between the two of them us," Michael thought.

Nick did not like this situation and convinced his parents to protest to Nikki. Nikki She assured them that all was alright and that they will only stay a day or two. On the day of her departure back to Nick's family, a huge snowstorm hit. They were snow bound, and they played house.

That night, Nikki asked Michael to sleep with her. He did. He held onto her but nothing more. He told her it would be wrong, and she agreed. The third day after the storm they ventured back to Manhattan. Nick was cold toward Michael and Nikki, but his parents were happy they were back. In the weeks that followed, Nikki and Michael talked about how they felt about each other. Michael asked her to marry him. She was so excited and just kept on kissing him.

Nikki called her parents to begin arrangements. Michael had to ask her father's permission, which he did over the phone. Nikki's mother and father were very generous and blessed them. Frances and Andy were in a state of shock, but happy. Michael told them the wedding would be in Cyprus in two months. They would have to buy their tickets on Olympic Airlines. Andy had to buy 20 tickets for the family. Nikki was preparing to leave for Cyprus, Michael took her to the airport. They were a beautiful couple. As the week's passed, Michael was all in for the wedding.

He ~~Michael~~ liked the darker side, and he would go down to the trucks in the village just to watch. He loved the edge, watching all those men dancing toward each other as if their movements were a ritual until they hooked onto someone. ~~He left.~~ Michael walked four blocks up to a quiet but classy bar and went in for a drink. ~~He~~ met Mark.

There he
Mark was a nice guy, and in an extremely excited voice, he asked Michael, "Do you know who was looking at you? That guy over there is a big playwright! Right there. Go over and talk to him."

Michael said, "I would rather talk to you." They did and hooked up that night.

124

Michael had a small apartment on Prospect Park West in Park Slope. Four floor walkup and the living room windows overlooked lower Manhattan and the building of the World Trade Center. This was a magnificent home for him and Nikki, which he told ~~Nikki~~ her in their nightly phone calls.

Nikki said, "Michael, my father wants to buy an apartment in the city for us."

Michael said, "Sure, but this is a starter."

As the weeks got closer to his departure, Michael started to get depressed, questioning his actions. "I am going to be a Reservoir Man," he thought. "I am going to hurt Nikki." Michael knew she would accept him as he was but realized that this was not the truth he always sought. Michael went into his bedroom and began undressing.

When Mark came into the room and asked him, "What's up babe?" Michael did not answer.

The next morning, he told Mark that he just wanted to be friends. "I am a better friend than being in a relationship."

Mark, feeling Michael was on the level, asked ~~Michael~~ him, "Can I borrow ten bucks as a friend?"

He looked at Michael, smiling "I would not ask if we were mates."

Michael laughed. The next few days, Michael went to work. He came home and sat on the park bench across from his apartment and ate pizza. He knew what he was doing by marrying Nikki was wrong. He went home to his parents and told them. As usual, they understood him and only wanted the best for him. He called Nick, who told Michael he was elated, but he assured Nick that there was no opening for him. He called Nikki in Cyprus, four days before the wedding, she understood. She understood Michael more than he imagined.

Michael got home to a phone call from Mark; he could not deal with his dog anymore. Mark asked if he could give Michael the dog and to hold him for a while.

"Sure," said Michael, "bring Charity over."

When Charity arrived, he fell in love with her. He knew he did the right thing; Charity was enough for him now. Nikki would always be a fond and loving memory for Michael, but he needed to find what would make him happy and complete.

126

Michael continued to be drawn to the darker side of the world, on an obsessive level. He went to the trucks at least twice a week, just to watch. He would patronize sex clubs but do nothing. Michael went walking down 42nd street below Broadway. All the john's and the hustlers were going to the movies—the cheapest and easiest way to hook up.

Michael would talk to the hustlers and the drag queens. Michael occasionally would go to Club 82 in the East Village on 4th Street to watch some great drag acts. After the show, he would sit in the empty audience waiting for them to come out. Some sat with him to talk, drink, and laugh. Michael would always hug them when they left.

He would tenderly say to them, "You are real."

On a cool night with a drizzle, Michael found himself back on 42nd Street. He had a need to be close with these hustlers, and then there was Davey in his leopard print pants coming on to Michael. Pushing Michael closer and closer to the hood of a parked car.

"Take me home. I will clean your house!" yelled Davey.

Michael passed on this opportunity. Suddenly, ~~Michael~~ he saw a man whom he could not place.

Davey interrupted Michael's gaze and said, "Leave him alone. He is a druggy. Sometimes he sleeps in the corner of that porn shop. Sad news!"

Michael walked over to him. ~~Michael~~ He knew him. God, it was Raphael from his first year at college. Michael asked him if he could help.

"Who the fuck are you, asshole? You want to go somewhere?" asked Raphael.

"No," said Michael, in shock. "But could we talk?"

"It will cost you," he responded.

"Your name is Raphael, you lived in Brooklyn, and you were an exchange student," said Michael.

"Close. My name is Peter, Pete, the guy with the big dick. Everything else you guessed is wrong. Give me ten bucks."

"I'm Michael. We went to school together, and we had that great night just talking. Please remember, please."

128

"If you say so," said Raphael. "The ten right here in my palm."

Michael stared at this broken man, wondering if he should have spent that night more intimately with Raphael. Things could have been different. Michael gave him the ten, gently kissing him.

"That will cost you," barked Raphael.

Michael stared at him, his face swelling with emotion, "It already has, Raphael, some of my soul." Michael saw the softness in Raphael's eyes for a moment, the kindness.

Michael thought, while walking to his train, "The journey to find yourself is long and some take the wrong roads, falling into despair. That desperation forces one to change sometimes for the better, but mostly for the worse. Desperation makes one take on separate roles in life so that one can easily forget the pain, the pain of who they are."

Michael walked to the F Train and at the token booth, there was Davey.

"Time to go," Michael said, "But not with me." Davey looked perplexed. Michael told him to go somewhere else and think.

"Go, walk uptown. Find a bench, sit by the river, ask, who is Davey? What makes Davey happy? Here is my phone number. When you find him, call me."

Michael knew this was not his road. Hollow sex, desperation, and drugs all leading to dead ends. Though Michael admired the Drag Queens; they saw truth within people and how things really were. He also admired the hustlers who could talk themselves into any john's arms and score. In the end, these men were the same as the Reservoir Men.

He understood he needed to leave this darker place behind. Their reality is moment to moment, only holding on to the next moment before it is gone. Michael knew his continued ramblings through life was finding him a greater truth and understanding. He saw the human condition in people. Michael was realizing now that all of us are on this journey together, simply choosing different paths.

CHAPTER ELEVEN

1971-1974

Michael rekindled his friendship with Mark. Mark, being a starving actor from Wisconsin, loved the theatre. Michael started a loving relationship with Charity, Mark's former dog. Charity was named after the Broadway musical "Sweet Charity." Mark's bond with Michael was teaching him about the theatre. They would second act Broadway shows, meaning they would walk in after the first act break with those who stepped outside for a smoke.

Michael was hooked. "Company," "Little Night Music," "70 girls 70," and "Follies." Michael saw "Company" seven times and Follies about ten. He chose to second act Follies only once because the balcony overhang was so steep it blocked the upper half of the stage when standing. Michael realized that the best seats in the house at the

Winter Garden were the first two rows of the mezzanine in the balcony.

Michael went to the theatre with anyone; he even took Frances to matinees on a regular basis. His mother would meet him on the 42nd street station of the 8th Avenue train. Frances climbed the stairs at 42nd Street, always commenting on the "poor souls" who lost their way. She was talking about the hustlers, prostitutes, pimps, and drag queens.

Michael would bow his head and say, "Sure, Mom."

Frances would not let it go, with comment after comment on the poor souls until they reached the theatre.

She talked so much that Michael was tempted to stop her in her tracks by saying, "Hey, Mom, I hang out there from time to time. I even met an old school mate!"

After the theatre, they went to the "China Bowl" on 44th Street and had Chinese food. Michael would walk her back to the train, making sure it was on the 44th street entrance. As time passed, there was little or no more talk of the 42nd street poor souls.

Mark did not have the luxury of a nice New York City paycheck, as Michael did. They started to get student rush tickets, which changed it all. This opened the flood gates and they never stopped going to the theatre. Student Rush was a half hour before curtain, where the producers would put a certain number of tickets on sale very cheaply for those with student ID's.

Mark asked Michael, "Why don't you go to school for theatre? City College has great programs."

Michael investigated the various programs at all the city colleges. He thought Brooklyn College had a solid MFA program, and they were not elitist. Michael took his transcript and made an appointment with the chairperson at the graduate school. The chairperson told Michael he had no background in theatre.

"You have three majors—English, History, and Philosophy, which doesn't add up to a background in theatre."

Michael was extremely disappointed. Dr. Riser, the chairperson, said to register for one class only in the graduate school, Stagecraft, to see if Michael liked it. There was a great professor teaching that class, and it touched on all aspects of practical theatre.

Michael registered for the class and found it challenging. Michael could not draw at all, so in set and costume design he was not particularly good. When it came to running crew, backstage or lights, Michael was there—and good.

Professor McGill talked to him, finding Michael's aggressiveness, thirst for knowledge, and intelligence extremely attractive. Michael and Professor McGill had a meeting with the chairperson: At the end of the meeting, Professor Riser shook his hand and welcomed Michael to the department.

Michael went home and called Mark. They opened a bottle of wine and talked theatre. Mark told Michael he was seeing someone from Georgia who was is in the Navy. Michael was happy for Mark, realizing a solid relationship is what Mark needed.

One night, at the bar 17 Barrow Street, a weird man came up to Michael. His name was Jack from Yonkers. He had a wig on but not a cheap one. He said he lived with his parents, who must have been 90, at least. He had a charm. They talked and exchanged numbers.

Jack loved "Hello Dolly." Phyllis Diller just came in as a replacement for the role of Dolly. Jack had great seats for Saturday and invited Michael.

"Sure, but just as friends," said Michael.

"No problem," said Jack.

Some of the restaurants did supper after the theatre. The curtain was at 8:30, so they got out about 11 at night. It was late, but Michael loved having dinner that late. He treated Jack to dinner, and this was the beginning of a new friendship.

Michael called Nick to tell him the good news about school. He left three messages on his answering machine; Nick never called back. Michael was so excited about starting graduate school, especially for a terminal degree—the MFA. Forty-five credits plus a thesis were the requirements to complete the degree.

The first semester, he took Directing 1, Stage Management, and History of American Theatre. He had the best of the faculty for those classes. He did very well his first semester and made an army of friends, including Joanne Smith and Flo Stein; the two of them became his best friends.

Michael invited all his new friends to his apartment to party, but the main attraction was an undergraduate student, Lenny. Lenny would borrow his mother's wig and dress. The dress fit him well, especially with his handlebar mustache. Lenny would lip sync "Leader of the Pack" sung by the group Shangri-Las. Lenny, as the years passed, became a good friend of Michael's. Lenny was one of a few friends that would cross over to Michael's other non-academic life. Lenny was lonely, and most classmates did not take him seriously; but Michael understood him.

The semester was terribly busy, and his directing assignments were overwhelming. Michael conquered them all. Michael hated acting, except when he was in the acting pool for other students' presentations, which he hated even more. He liked the technical work and was master electrician for "Jacque Brel is Alive and Well," which was a senior thesis project for an undergraduate.

Jacque Brel was now second only to Dylan as his favorite songwriter/singer. He learnt about Yiddish Theatre and how it was the basis of American Musical Theatre. In his class was Dianne, one of the leading actresses in Yiddish Theatre. She invited him to several of her performances, and he loved it even though he did not know what was

136

being said. He and Dianne became good school friends.

Michael's Directing Professor, Rae, liked him and invited him to his house for brunch. Rae made the best omelets. Rae taught at the Cours Florent in Paris, one of France's most prestigious drama schools. Michael learnt a lot from Rae over numerous brunches. They would talk about the role of the director and his relationship with the actor. Rae also knew so many people that were famous. Michael enjoyed those stories the best. Rae would occasionally ask Michael to go to bed with him. Michael avoided that conversation as much as possible. Rae saw the honesty in Michael and stopped asking. But Jack, that guy with the wig who saw "Hello Dolly" with Michael, had a good friend who liked older men. Michael hooked Jack's friend up with Rae.

Michael, after being at the school for a semester, knew it was time for his interview with the Dean of the School, Professor Eliott Long. He made his appointment. Dean Long only taught one class a semester, Theatre Management. His background was authoring several books, running a large summer theatre on Cape Cod, and hosting high level seminars that became books, including Producing and Directing.

Michael was nervous. He walked into a huge office and sat down far from his desk. Eliott walked in. He was a nice-looking man about forty or so. Eliott was White Anglo Saxon and very elite. He smoked with bravado, which made him a bit affected. They talked about everything, most of which Michael forgot. At the end of the conversation, Eliott got up, shook Michael's hand, and welcomed him to the school.

As Michael was leaving his office, Dean Long stopped him, and said, "I will have a few students at my home on Saturday night, hoping you can come. My secretary will give you my address and phone number, only use if you get lost."

Michael made it to Dean Long's penthouse apartment in Brooklyn Heights. Everywhere you stood in the apartment, you saw Manhattan out the windows. His terrace overlooked lower Manhattan and on the right side was the Empire State Building. Eliott greeted Michael with a big smile and introduced him to the other students, some of which he knew.

"What do you want to drink?" Eliott asked.

"Just a beer," replied Michael.

"What? Beer? Are you serious? Not on a Saturday evening!" said Eliott.

Eliott continued, "No, the drink of a successful man is vodka. Now you can have a Greyhound, Screwdriver, or a Cape Cod. You, Michael are a Cape Cod, sweet and strong."

Michael really enjoyed the Cape Cod, and he had about three before he left. A bit tipsy, he thanked Eliott and started to leave the party.

Eliott turned to him and said, "You'll be back. You have a lot to learn, and you make good company."

Michael smiled and replied, "looking forward to it."

Mark and his new friend Wade were frequent visitors to Michael's home. Mark seemed a bit uncomfortable with Wade in their last visit. Michael liked Wade and found him honest and sensitive. Wade was not that book smart but had good instincts. He liked Michael and would always talk to him. One day, out of nowhere, Mark broke off his friendship with Wade. Michael came home from work and found Wade in his hallway crying.

Michael looked at Wade and said, "Come on up. I have a bottle of wine, and I'll order a pizza."

Michael did not want to pursue any form of a relationship with Wade because of his friendship with Mark. Michael's quest was to free Wade from the Navy and his provincial southern roots. Wade's father beat him badly, and he had huge scars on his leg and back.

Michael did help Wade get out of the Navy, honorably, and he started Jr. College at ~ *spell out* Kingsborough in Brooklyn. After discharge, he slept on Michael's couch and had no intention of leaving. Michael did not care. He was still able to hook up with people, he was happy, and Wade felt secure.

Michael was a leader in the Performing Arts Department. He was able to secure a small space at the college for the MFA students to mount small productions. He was at the end of his degree requirements. His master's thesis was on T.S. Elliot, so he mounted a production of "Murder in the Cathedral" off campus and produced it with funds he raised. He even gave Mark a nice role. The production was extremely successful.

His relationship with Dean Long grew but sometimes in the wrong direction. Dean Long was
140

getting extremely aggressive, wanting to sleep with Michael. Michael pleaded that it would be wrong, and Dean Long listened. However, it got worse on every visit to his house. Dean Long did plant a dream in Michael, somehow, that he should start a Regional Theatre.

Michael thought that a Regional Theatre would be a great idea and got to work. He met with Joanne and Flo. Michael was friendly with someone at the Rockefeller Foundation who gave him a box of multiple cards called "Cemeral Theatre Games" for students. This program was developed by the Rockefeller Foundation, and it was great. His friend told Michael he could use this, promotionally, as part of his Regional Theatre program.

Michael invited Joanne and Flo to the house. He told them about his proposal to go to a middle size town like Lincoln, Nebraska, or Augusta, Georgia, and develop a theatrical season, plan acting classes for the community, and go into the public school with the Cemeral Program. He knew Tom Gallo, who was very connected with community-based groups in the United States like the Junior League and the Women's Club.

Gallo made the introduction to the Junior League, and Michael asked for help. Tom also gave

Michael contacts with the University of Georgia in case he decided to go to Georgia. Michael knew that if Wade got back to Georgia, having family there, he could complete his four-year degree and bond with them. Well, it was Augusta or bust!

The group made phone calls to the Junior League, Augusta College, Women's Club, and many civic organizations. The reaction was great. They decided to go to Augusta on a preliminary visit. They set up appointments. Joanne was to go with Michael and Wade to share the driving.

Andy and Frances had no problem with Michael going, and Andy bought Michael a new car, a Dodge Swinger, making him look more *Karmann* businesslike, as opposed to his ~~Carmen~~ Ghia. They began their journey in Michael's new car, and it only took them thirteen hours via US 95 to Columbia, South Carolina, then a short drive on US 20 to Augusta.

In Augusta, they stayed at the Bon Aire Hotel, an old antebellum luxury hotel which aged in time. They took their meetings and had a wonderful time. Augusta College agreed to house them to mount their productions. All the civic clubs greeted them with an offer to help. The hotel they were staying at agreed to give them office space.

Michael thought they now had the foundation of a Regional Theatre. A member of the Women's Club offered Michael a carriage house with four bedrooms for free, and now, they had a home. They were ready to head back with a quick stop in Atlanta to meet with an executive from the State Board of Education.

Michael was able to secure a pleasant hotel on Peachtree Street. Mr. Stevenson, Assistant Director of the Board of Education for Georgia, was one hour late. Michael and Joanne were on their second wine, feeling loose and limber. Mr. Stevenson arrived and explained to them there were grants available for the Performing Arts, and he would be happy to help them attempt to secure a grant.

The meeting was ending just as Mr. Stevenson grabbed Michael at the bar, telling him, "You are an extremely attractive young man. I am staying at the hotel for the night, and I would appreciate your company in my room."

Michael excused himself and walked over to Joanne.

Michael told her, "He wants to sleep with me, I guess in exchange for a grant. I am going over there to tell him it was an honor but no!"

143

Joanne told Michael "Go, it means money for us and maybe more!"

Michael got incredibly angry and said, "You are fucking crazy. You want me to go with a Reservoir Man? How can you even suggest this?"

Joanne was very defensive and said, "What is a Reservoir Man? What are you saying? Do what you want!"

Michael then walked over to Mr. Stevenson and told him it was an honor to meet him, but he must get up early in the morning to head back to New York. Michael walked out of the lounge and found a bench on Peachtree Street.

Joanne came out of the lounge looking for Michael. She found him sitting on a bench looking terribly upset and sad. She bent over him and kissed him on the head.

"I am sorry Michael. I'm so sorry for hurting you."

Michael looked at her saying, "This happens so often to me. I do not understand. I don't think I am that attractive, ~~my mother does though~~."

Joanna looked at him, with a smile, and said, "Michael, ~~I will tell you from what I see, and~~ I

144

think a few other girls at school would have agreed. You have sexy hazel eyes, you're tall, your physique is strong, your chest is hairy, there's the scar on your lip, your complexion, and your masculinity. That is it! No, you are not a Rock Hudson or even an Omar Shariff, but boy, are you sexy. You get it? This is your calling card. It is what you were born with. Okay? Also, most of these older men make plays for younger guys putting themselves in a vulnerable position to get action. If they try to hire an escort, it could be a huge scandal if it ~~gets~~ got out, especially if they are known and respected in their community. Let's get coffee, find Wade and Flo, and get ready to go home."

Michael was satisfied with Joanne's speech about his physical appearance, but he was really hoping Joanne would say they wanted him for his intellect and perception of life. Michael returned a kiss on Joanne's head.

Michael did not utter one word driving home. He understood what Joanne said, but Michael found it funny that he never took a second look in the mirror in the morning. Every time an aunt or her friends would say, "What a good-looking boy," he never thought twice about what they said. Well, it is what it is, thought Michael.

Michael knew he needed to worry about his regional theatre.

Michael planned his first season; he would open with Tennessee Williams' "Glass Menagerie." He was fond of the play and spent a great weekend meeting Williams at Cape Cod, Mass. while they *spell out* were producing the premiere of William's "Small Craft Warnings" at Eliott's theatre. Following "Glass Menagerie" was "Merry Wives of Windsor," Anouilh's "Antigone," and "Front Page." What Michael loved about the character of Antigone was her loyalty. Michael instinctively believed that loyalty was an element in the human condition that we might be losing.

Ticket sales looked good; Michael was back at the civic clubs selling tickets. There was one major element missing—his board of directors was not raising money for the theatre. The Vice Chairman of the Board, Clarence Joy, had connections with the governor. They got a private plane and flew to Atlanta. ~~It was a one engine prop plane, and it was very scary flying~~.

The Chairman of the Board, Kurt Baldwin, was African American and a great guy. He was as afraid of flying in the plane as Michael was. They got to the governor's mansion and sat in his room.

one-engine prop

There were twenty cubicles in the round, and they sat where they were assigned.

The doors opened and the Governor and his aide went from one cubical to another. When he came to Michael's cubicle, the Governor stared at him Michael. He offered his hand with the broadest smile Michael had ever seen in his life, like that of a future president. Michael walked out with ten thousand dollars. The flight home was joyous, and he felt like he was flying in a 747 jet.

The theatre was ready to open in two months. The Cemeral school program began in limited classrooms. Michael had to go up to New York to begin casting "Merry Wives of Windsor" with his guest director. He was in for the weekend, there wanting to spend time with his family. Michael was casting actors on Monday and Tuesday.

He called Eliott, telling him of all the wonderful things happening to the theatre. Eliott insisted he come over to the apartment for an early evening drink. Michael was so proud of what he accomplished he could not wait to tell Eliott everything. Michael got there about 6 pm, and Eliott had a Greyhound waiting for him as well as a little dinner. But it should have been a Cape Cod. Michael took a second drink, a Cape Cod. Michael was not feeling too well, and he did not understand that only two drinks would make him feel so dizzy.

Michael woke up in bed with Eliott, not remembering anything. The first clear memory was Eliott's companion standing in the doorway of the bedroom smiling at an almost naked Michael.

Michael got up and said, "I ~~get~~ have to go. My parents are expecting me."

Eliott gave him a cup of coffee and a bun of some sort. Michael saw the Sunday Times on the table in the living room. It was two days later. He ran out of the apartment and found a phone booth to call his mother. Michael told her how sorry he was that he was a few days late seeing them.

"It is Sunday, so you made macaroni?" asked Michael.

His mother responded, "Yes, I did."

Michael was directing "Glass Menagerie" and had a great company of actors. The Junior League planned a great opening party in a huge gazebo in downtown Augusta. Everyone was there, even Andy and Frances who came to support their son. The play opened to great reviews from the local papers and TV critics.

148

Michael was also having a thing with his lead actor, Rod. This was a bad move. Michael was confident of the potential success of the theatre. No one was living in the company house, but they secured their own apartments. Wade was looking to resettle with his family in Macon, Georgia.

Things seemed settled for a minute except for one minor problem for Michael. Eliott began writing him love letters saying things that made Michael extremely uncomfortable. He finally found the courage to call Eliott, asking him to stop. He left the message on his answering machine. Eliott never responded. Michael did not understand how the Dean of a prestigious school would put himself in a compromising position. Michael thought Eliott was a Reservoir Man, but of a higher order. He did not want to think about this too much.

The theatre was running out of money while "Merry Wives," was in rehearsal. Michael met with the Board, who asked Michael to call his family for additional funds. The Board members did not contribute one penny of their own money. Andy said he would cover any tax money due to the federal government, but the Board had to produce something. One by one they resigned within a 24-hour period. Michael was holding the bag, while left everyone left, even Joanne. Michael told the actors their paychecks were in the bond held by Actor's Equity.

Andy sent ~~down~~ enough money to fly the actors back to New York and for Michael to make arrangements to come home. Rod stayed with Michael at the apartment, and Wade was Missing in Action. The company owed little money except ~~for~~ to a lumber supplier who was threatening Michael. Rod told Michael it was getting a little tense. He needed to get home~~, so he did~~.

Michael hired a truck and put all his belongings ~~in the truck~~ into it. He stayed for a few days with Bess, an older woman, who lived two counties over from Augusta. Michael met Bess when he first came to the area~~, and she lived far enough away from the lumber man~~.

Tom Gallo gave Michael a lead on a job in upstate New York, where they were restoring a hundred-year-old theatre building to house a regional theatre. The guy up there, Jesse Reed, knew little about running a theatre company. Michael called him, and they hit it off. He decided to go up and meet him. Michael was feeling a bit more secure with the prospect of a job and a new opportunity, but first, he had to head home.

Rod came to Michael's parents' house and walked with Michael on the boardwalk. They sat on a bench, and Michael told Rod that the relationship must end. Michael had a lot of affection for him, but it was not the right time. Rod was devastated, but ~~and so, they shook hands~~. ~~Rod~~ thanked him and walked away. When Michael got back to the house, he got a phone call from Wade, who left his family and wanted to meet Michael. Since Michael's car was still in Georgia at Bess' house, Wade was able to drive the car back to New York.

The next day, Michael immediately left for upstate New York driving his father's car. Jesse, the cultural planner at the theatre and the city's cultural planning ~~commission~~ commissioner, met with Michael. After a few hours, they offered him the job. Michael asked them for a few days but was extremely interested. His hesitation was that Jesse had more bravado than substance. He was a nice guy, as was his wife, and both were actors.

~~Being~~ Back at his parents' house, Michael thought how it was good that there was not a big mess left in Georgia. He decided to call Eliott ~~for help~~ to see if he knew if there were any other jobs that Michael may qualify for before accepting the job at the theatre. Dover was great, but he was worried about Jesse's lack of knowledge. Eliott

151

came to the phone, and Michael asked him for any referrals for jobs. Eliott simply said, "You had your fifteen minutes in the sun. Michael, get a shovel and dig ditches like your kind does so well."

CHAPTER TWELVE

1975-1979

Michael was ready to go to Dover. His truck was filled with furniture and sitting in front of his parents' home. Wade was driving his car directly to the theatre. He also did not tell Michael any of his intentions once he reached Dover.

Michael secured a ~~an~~ two-bedroom apartment in Smithville, a small town outside of Dover. ~~It had two bedrooms~~. He knew Wade's suitcase would drop at his front door. He liked Wade and felt he would make a good companion, especially in this unfamiliar environment.

Wade took the second bedroom gleefully. Wade was motivated, though he always took his time. This time, he made it happen within two weeks. He secured a job at a medical lab drafting reports and enrolled at a college where he still would have three years to graduate. ~~He lost so~~

many credits in the transfer, he had great grades. Wade was settled to go on with life.

Michael spent a week alone with Jesse, the artistic director and cultural planner, talking about the future of the operation. There was still a considerable amount of work to be done in the restoration of the ceiling. Michael was also called a cultural planner, which he was extremely uncomfortable with since that title had nothing to do with producing theatre.

The City of Dover was deemed an All-American City and given grants by the federal government to beautify and restore its 19th century architecture. The restoration of the theatre became a major objective, along with many other projects.

A painter for the ceiling was hired, David Lin and his assistant, both from France. The scaffolding was placed, covering the entire ceiling, and painting began. Four months later, Michael had advanced his goals in theatre planning. Michael was able to prepare a budget, begin a dialogue with Actor's Equity, and start hiring an administrative staff. After all this time, the ceiling was still not done. The architects had completed most of their work but were holding out on completion until the painters were done.

Finally, they were ready to go. The first season's opening play was "London Assurance" (which originally opened the theatre one hundred years ago), then Wade Dos Passos's "USA," followed by the musical "Babes in Arms," and closing with "Dracula." ~~Dover was an old mill town,~~ ~~but~~ The townspeople were incredibly supportive of the theatre. Dover was part of a TriCity area rich in history.

Subscription sales were disappointing. Jesse, now Artistic Director, was holding out ~~beyond~~ hope that they would do well once the season opened. Jesse knew little about producing, and Michael hoped his artistic knowledge was outstanding.

Michael was very content with himself. Two days before the opening of the theatre, everything was in order. Michael put together a great staff. Jesse did not want to have previews, so there was no room for errors. The show was sold out—all 500 seats.

Michael had a few days to be alone before opening. He went up to the Dover Falls, the same place where, according to legend among the Dover

155

people, Hiawatha committed suicide by going over the falls. He had a great bench looking directly at the huge falls. Michael could not bury Eliott's remarks. They hurt him. Eliott meant a lot to Michael, but he was cast aside so cruelly. ~~Michael~~ He also had to contend with the shadowy memories he had of those two nights at Eliott's apartment. He decided he was not going to feel sorry for himself and that, most importantly, Eliott was only a higher-class Reservoir Man. It was sad how some people did not let friendships develop, letting small obstacles stand in the way. Michael would not let insignificant obstacles interfere in his life, not here in Upstate, New York.

There was a that ~~great~~ bar and restaurant in Dover. Michael would go before every show and have a Cape Cod. He walked back to the theatre, feeling great. Michael checked the Box Office; all tickets were sold. He went upstairs into the theatre to check with the House Manager. No riots. Everything was in order, and there was a general feeling of anticipation. ~~All was ready for the show to begin~~. The audience was chatty and anxious for the play to start.

There was a great ovation at the end of the play, but a reviewer pointed out the ovation was more for the facility and the restoration ~~then~~ than the

156

play itself. Michael thought that was mean. The problem with the mixed reviews for the play was Jesse's inability to have a good relationship with the critics.

The second production did worse. Jon Dos Pasos's "USA" was interesting from a historical point of view. Jesse directed this one as well, and he was roasted again. The production felt more like a library presentation than a play. The Chairman of the Board phoned Michael and requested him to come to his office. He asked Michael what he thought of Jesse's creative ability. Michael said that as a person, Jesse was great, but as an artistic administrator, he had not been with Jesse long enough to make a judgement. As Michael left the meeting, he wondered how he could even answer the question with his own lack of artistic experience? He liked Jesse and did not want to hurt him.

Jesse did not direct the next show, "Babes in Arms," which was a musical. The director, who Jesse hired, was not particularly good. He put twenty-three chorus dancers and principal actors on a small stage at the same time. It was insane to say the least. The production was laughable. Jesse was fired at an emergency meeting with the board.

Michael found Jesse in near tears later that night in the theatre. Jesse did not understand why he was fired. He asked Michael if he had a hand in it. ~~getting him fired.~~ Michael explained the conversation he ~~had~~ had with the chairperson and how he supported Jesse as much as he could. Jesse and his wife did not believe Michael, though ~~Michael~~ he had nothing to do with the decision. Jesse left the theatre quickly with his wife to go to their home in Chicago.

The final production was "Dracula," but a director was never hired. The author, who was very well-known, liked Michael and told him he would direct it. Since the author knew the script so well, it took a lot of pre-production burden off the staff. There were many special effects such as bats flying, fog rolling, and blood spraying. The production was great. All twenty-six performances were sold out. The Board was ecstatic and told Michael they wanted him to be Artistic Director next season.

The State Art's council had their own agenda, and it did not involve Michael. With the money purse in their hands, they urged the board to hire Tony Drew, a Musical Theatre director and composer. They did. Michael remained Managing Director. Tony, the new director, chose a season with two of his own musicals. Michael felt that was wrong since the theatre's job was to serve a community, not a director to have his shows produced.

The season, other than his two musicals, had great choices like "Vanities," "Subject was Roses," and "Abbie's Irish Rose." The reviews were much better, but Tony never came to board meetings nor Executive Board meetings. First week on the job, Tony hit a deer on the New York Thruway. Suddenly, Tony was paranoid of deers and driving to the theatre, and his irrational fear of them made it impossible to attend board meetings.

With or without his phobia, he had no personal stake in the community nor the theatre, which was the pride of Dover. Tony resigned. The board asked Michael to take over. Michael was genuinely liked by the community as well as the board members, the theatre's Ladies' Guild, and the ex-female mayor of Dover. ~~Ellen~~

Michael accepted the offer. He came back to the apartment with a bottle of wine, excited to tell Wade. As he approached the apartment door, he heard loud music. He opened the door to find three naked men and Wade having a wonderful time. Wade told Michael to join in, but Michael declined.

"They aren't my type," said Michael. "The party is over guys. Next time," said Michael, shooing them out.

He told Wade that he should get his own apartment. Wade asked Michael if he could hold off for a while. Michael said in two months, three maybe. They opened the wine and had a quiet but nice night. They listened to sitar music and a little Chet Baker.

As the evening wore on, Wade, less than sober, said, "You know, Michael, what your problem is? You help so many people. Some of them get emotionally involved, and you both act on a whimsical feeling. After you help them, you lose interest. You are a wonderful man who has helped so many people."

Michael then said, "What about you? I helped you get out of the Navy, and nothing happened between us."

"Exactly," said Wade. "I knew there was more to come, and your friendship was more important than a roll ~~or more~~ in the hay."

Michael looked at Wade and said, "You're drunk!"

Michael moved to Huntsville, and Wade went on his own to the downtown area. Michael knew he would miss Wade's friendship. When they went out for dinner. Wade would not say a word because starting a conversation was hard for Wade. This gave Michael the perfect excuse to phase out and think about his next adventure.

Michael always believed that his phasing out, which happened often, was attributed to the drugs his cousin gave him for the lack of dopamine in his brain. Michael did not like focusing on this. When friends asked why he appeared to be somewhere else, "It is what it is. We need to go on." he would say

Michael loved his new apartment because it was a condominium on a lake. The other apartments were not nearby. Since an early age, Michael always had a problem with clothes. He hated wearing them, and this apartment gave him the excuse and the freedom not to wear them.

Michael began forming a company of actors for the coming season. He relied on Julliard and Yale graduates to build the company. He was to

open the third season with "Glass Menagerie," *Stapleton*
which he would direct. Maureen ~~Stapelton~~ was
interested since she was born and raised in Troy,
New York, but she attempted to change Michael's
choice of "Glass Menagerie" to a restoration
comedy with sixteen roles and an expensive
production budget. Michael met her for drinks in
Troy, where she closed the book on "Glass
Menagerie" because she could not take the pain of
another gentleman caller leaving. Her agent at ICM
recommended Maureen O'Sullivan of Tarzan
fame, ~~she was the first Jane~~. O'Sullivan was also
the mother of Mia Farrow and the husband of the
famous producer and director John Farrow.
Michael met with her and really hit it off. *they*

   Maureen opened the season to
extraordinary reviews. Several powerful people in
the theatrical industry came to the theatre to see
the production and the incredible building. Michael
was off to a great start, and the other productions
were just as successful. He cast Kaiulani Lee and
Wade DeVries, two extremely popular actors for
Eugene O'Neill's "Moon for the Misbegotten,"
which attracted several New York critics.

   Ticket sales were great, but donations were *good*
not as ~~great~~ as they hoped. The grants from both
the state and federal government were larger, but *had*
162

the Board had hoped for more. Michael developed a film series on Monday nights with a local newspaper film and theatre critic, which was extraordinarily successful.

His Tuesday night concert series was also successful. The series attracted such amazing talent as Oscar Brand, the folk singer, and Valerie Harper with Anthony Zerbe performing "Love Letters." Others included Geraldine Fitzgerald, Emmanuel Axe, The Gilbert and Sullivan Quartet, and Anna Russell, an opera singer with a rock star following, she performed sort of parody on opera. Michael had a well-developed regional theatre and felt artistically satisfied with the theatre and himself.

Michael got many small awards from the community, but his favorite one was from his staff. During a pizza party, they honored him as "Best Employer." He was also named in "Who's Who" as a business leader. Michael was asked to produce a play at the Egg in Albany, the performing Arts Center for New York State that just recently opened. It was designed by IM Pie. Dover would be the first professional performance at the Egg.

Michael received a great script submitted to him by a young playwright from Cleveland based on Dickens's "A Christmas Carol." Dickens, being a thespian, wrote "A Christmas Carol" with his acting troupe in mind. Dickens invited his acting company for Christmas Eve dinner. They all arrived at his home and were escorted to his attic, which had sliding ladders and secret doors perfect to act out his play. Dickens gave out parts of the novel to be acted out by his company of fellow actors. The production was an extraordinary hit.

Michael received a letter from Harvard University asking him to join other arts leaders from all disciplines for a series of classes and lectures lasting two months. The seminars included sections discussing the relationship of the community to the arts institution, ~~Other seminars,~~ the Creative Environment, and managing the arts as a business. The Board graciously told Michael to go. Michael asked ~~Andy~~ his father for the money, reminding him he said he would always pay for education and health expenses, ~~and Andy said, "You are right." Michael was going.~~ The University would house participants in the dorms. Michael, in his total need for privacy, rented his set designer's apartment in Back Bay.

Michael was ready to leave for Boston. Wade, of course, stayed at his apartment and watched all three dogs. ~~Michael~~ He arrived in Back Bay; the apartment was just across the street from the Charles River.

164

Michael enjoyed lunch and the coffee break where he got to talk to many managers from other artistic disciplines. ~~He made it a point to have dinner and coffee with them~~. He learned a lot about the creative environment, managing and the relationship with the Board of Directors and their responsibility.

There was one student, ~~that~~ (a red headed male) never stopped looking at him during the class. ~~He had red hair.~~ This gentleman always had a few fellow classmates hovering over him. Michael found out he came from an upper crust family from Boston. He invited Michael to a party he was having at his home. A fellow student who hung out with Michael told him he was going to a blue blood party. Michael knew his invitation was more than a meet and greet. He dressed very well and went off to the party.

When he got to the address, he sat on a nearby bench and watched the guests going into a large brownstone house. Michael decided to head home. ~~This was a huge problem with Michael~~. He did not feel worthy to be around the type of upper-class people who were ~~heading~~ there ~~into the house~~. Did Eliott nail it when he said that Michael was just made to dig ditches?

At the end of the program, the school threw a great party and dinner. The car ride home was an awakening for Michael. He was extremely uncomfortable with people of a higher social bracket. He now understood why he loved Dover and his staff, who were all like him. It was the same in Augusta. He got along better with the Women's Club versus the Junior League.

Michael fit in with people who were everyday types because he found them to be more honest and loyal. After arriving home, he went directly to the theatre, then upstairs to the lobby. He was greeted by his staff with a big "Welcome Home" sign and what looked like ten pizzas ready to be eaten. Michael shared beer and pizza with them late into the night.

Michael asked his staff how they knew he would come directly to the theatre when he arrived. They answered, "Where else would you go? If you did not come here first, we would quit!" Michael realized this was a group of young people that accepted his lifestyle unconditionally. Unfortunately, this was not the case with society overall; Dover was special.

This bond with his staff was created out of respect for Michael and how hard he worked believed and respected in each of them. Their enthusiasm toward Michael was demonstrated in how hard they worked to successfully have him listed in "Who's Who in America."

At the little welcome home party, Michael's business manager introduced him to his new master electrician, Ben. Michael and Ben sat in a corner and talked. Michael asked him his age; and he was twenty-four.

Michael stared at him, "And you think you could run my lights?"

Ben looked at Michael, with a smile, and said, "Easy, boss."

Ben came from a lower income family, but he was skilled. Michael liked him, and they became friends through the next whole season.

The Season was an extraordinary success: "A Christmas Carol," "Candida," and "Agatha Christie's The Unexpected Guest." When the season ended, Michael spent the summer around the upstate area. Michael received an unexpected phone call from a gentleman named Al Coffee who happened to be chairperson of the theatre department at the State University. He invited Michael for coffee at his office. Michael accepted, and they had a wonderful time together. Al asked Michael to join his faculty as an adjunct. Michael felt great about this new adventure and challenge.

There were several Theatre Arts Leaders who believed Michael did not belong in the position at the theatre. They called his chairperson of the Board several times, indicating there were more appropriate Artistic Directors that would give the theatre a higher visibility and lead to greater funding.

Several things ~~What~~ saved Michael's position ~~were several things~~. The Board respected Michael as an administrator and for his passion. ~~and~~ They acknowledged his love for the people of Dover. Also, Michael ~~did not have one negative~~ had no critical review from anything he directed in his two seasons. ~~He proved to be solely in charge~~. Finally, there was the constant and harmonious productivity of the theatre staff. Michael spent a good deal of time with Al that summer. Al slowly attempted to convince him to move the theatre to the campus. ~~He would attempt to talk to the~~ and talk with the authorities at the university ~~to help erase~~ about erasing the theatre's fund balance deficit.

Michael realized how attracted he was to Ben, ~~his new electrician~~ but was afraid to act. They

168

took a day trip together, as they often did, checking out lighting equipment. They stopped at one of the many lakes in the upstate area and had lunch that Michael had prepared. ~~Michael often brought his lunch everywhere and always brought his lunch to work at the theatre.~~ Michael responded to Ben's honesty and his effortless way of looking at life. His thoughts were easy and ~~so~~ beautiful. The lazy, sizzling summer never ended, nor did his feelings toward Ben.

Michael was getting ready for the sixth season, which included "Arsenic and Old Lace," "Runner Stumbles," "Death of a Salesman," Murray Schisgal's "Luv," and a world premier play. ~~Michael~~ He was hoping that this coming winter was not like the last when the metro area had one hundred eighty inches of snow. Even in that much snow, ticket buyers still came, and only two shows were cancelled all season. Michael was positive that they were in for a great season.

Michael gave his first interview with the press about the coming season. During the interview, ~~Michael~~ he stated that he felt the stage at the Music Hall was too small, and had no wing space. Everything had to fly by sandbags on and off the stage. It limited the scope of the productions. In addition, the set had to be constructed, no bigger with than six feet pieces, ~~it~~ which had to be brought up two ~~large~~ flights of stairs as there was no loading dock. Over the ~~The~~ next two days, the press made it seem like the theatre was planning to move. One reporter caught up with Al ~~at school~~. Al told ~~the reporter~~ him he would love to help the theatre company and give it a new home.

~~Michael was directing the first play,~~ When coming out of rehearsal, ~~he found~~ Michael the press and TV cameras waiting outside. This caught him off guard, and he did not have the right answers for them. The local people could not understand how the building would go to the university. This continued all during rehearsal.

"Runner Stumbles" opened with the most critical praise of all the six seasons. The lines outside the box office were extraordinary. The success of the production covered up the tension created by the talks of a potential move. Michael felt like he betrayed the community. The Board ~~meeting was chaotic. They~~ now passed a resolution that the theatre company would stay in Dover, and the idea of a residency at the University was dead.

Michael left for New York on a break. He and Ben stayed at a tenement building in the East Village on the fourth floor. The bathtub was in a small kitchen, but the fire escape was the best. They stayed at the apartment for four days and did not come out except to eat. It was the apartment of his technical director, and it had a great aura. When Michael left to get back to Dover, he felt as if he just left a spa in the Caribbean.

Coming back to Dover, he now faced another problem. Al with feeding the press a lot of false information, the press was now saying that Michael was going to leave the Music Hall and develop a new theatre company at the University. Michael told the press this was not true; his loyalty to Dover was solid. Michael knew it was time for it to be over, and he submitted his resignation to the Board.

There was no pleading by anyone except the staff for Michael to stay. Michael, the community, and the Board knew it was time for him to go. A search committee was formed, and Michael was made vice chair of the committee. In the following days, Michael told Ben he could not go with him; it was better that he established his own life. Wade was moving with him; Michael had secured an apartment in Park Slope. Ben understood and hugged Michael. Michael knew Ben was an Everyman in all meanings of the word.

The Board had a challenging time finding a replacement. ~~All the funding sources turned their backs on them since they did not listen to them years ago.~~ Michael knew leaving Ben behind completed the circle that made the magic of Dover. The day he was leaving, Ben came to the apartment with a boxed lunch and lots of hugs. Michael got into the car and drove off, never looking back. He would always love Ben.

CHAPTER THIRTEEN

1979-1982

Michael and Wade were having a quiet evening together, sipping a ~~great~~ bottle of wine in their ~~a fantastic~~ duplex apartment in Park Slope. Wade always felt indebted to Michael; he would not have seen or done any of these adventures on his own. ~~Michael knew Wade was a great friend.~~ Michael was happy to see that Wade landed an excellent job at an international drug company writing lab reports. Wade had a great salary, which made Michael secure since his income was nonexistent.

Michael put on an Edith Piaf album he had bought in Dover. ~~Their evening became more mellow.~~ Wade asked Michael why he didn't let Ben move in with him. Though Wade was happy to be living with Michael, he still had to question it.

Michael looked at Wade sadly and answered, "Right now, I have nothing but great memories of my life. Why take Ben on a journey that might go into chaos? ~~He might get a survival job that would last a few years, any career would go nowhere.~~" Michael continued, "It was not right, and it was hard on me to not be with him. I have not spoken to him ~~at all~~ since I left Dover. It is better this way~~, right now I don't know what would have happened if he moved in.~~"

Wade looked at Michael, "I always see you ~~take second position for the betterment of the person next to you.~~ put others first. You always go out of your way to help people, but your reward is very slim."

Michael shrugged his shoulders, looking away. "The reward is seeing a friend having an excellent job, graduating college, and being free, as in your case. You are right, I helped many people who afterward disappeared. ~~Suddenly, I am off doing my next adventure.~~ I helped them that is all that matters."

Wade got up and came over to Michael, kissing him on the cheek. ~~Wade looked into Michael's eyes.~~ Looking into Michael's eyes, Wade said, "You are the best."

174

"You are the best," said Wade.

"~~Sure~~, Sometimes," Michael answered, drifting into the echoes of Piaf.

Michael had to ~~really~~ figure out how to earn some money. He started preliminary work on a business plan for a talent agency. He had three fantasies of jobs outside of the industry: driving a cab, working construction, and being a chorus member. The chorus member was out since he had no practical experience. His uncle Pattie owned a large electrical contracting company, ~~Michael~~ but Michael ~~struck out there too; he~~ did not have the credentials to apprentice on a job for union credit.

Driving a cab might be ~~great~~ good. He contacted a car service company near his family home and started ~~to work~~ working. ~~The guys~~ Michael thought the guys on the two-way dispatch radio were a bunch of "neo-Nazi pigs." ~~Michael~~ He loved that term and used it often. He ~~both~~ lasted ~~prevailed and endured~~ at the cab company for six weeks. These guys knew where the weirdos lived when they called in for a cab. They made sure Michael got ~~the~~ those calls—from drunks, nasty people, people who could not speak English, and finally, a lot of smelly kids laughing and abusing one another.

The radio dispatch guys told Michael, "This call is for you. You will love this woman."

Michael did not know what to expect. He picked up a young woman, and she appeared normal. She smiled and got in the car.

"Take me to Kennedy."

Michael quoted her the price, and he then Proceeded to the airport. As he was driving, he felt a piece of paper hit him in the back of the head. The young woman told him to take it. She told him she had a hotel room reserved at the airport. The piece of paper was a hundred-dollar bill.

Returning the money Michael responded quickly, "Sorry I'm working and have lots of obligations tonight."

She retorted, "Work on me, we can do this quick."

Michael stopped at the hotel she requested.

OK   As she got out, she threw him the 100 dollars and said, "Thanks, cutie."

ok ~~Michael took the hundred~~. As she was closing the door, Michael said, "The fare is 25 dollars to the airport."

The woman reluctantly gave him the 25 dollars and said, "Here you go, I'll get you next time."

Michael said to himself, "No, you will not. I will not be ~~here~~ on this job." Michael thought she ~~must be~~ probably was into some funky stuff, like killing him in the hotel room or heavy sex. Michael drove back to the cab company, dropped off his fares, and was ready to leave. The dispatcher asked if he had a fun time.

"The best," Michael answered, had ~~with the 100 dollars in his pocket~~.

Michael parked his car two blocks from the house. He was tired and was frazzled with ~~his~~ the trip to the airport. As he was walking home, he noticed a young, good-looking man in a van. He was smiling at Michael. Michael thought he might have known him. As he approached the driver's door, the young man slowly brought his arm through the driver side window, ~~where.~~ He was wearing solid brass knuckles.

Michael said, "Look buddy, I just had this crazy woman giving me a hundred dollars. I'm not giving it up, no way."

As he said that he realized the young good-looking gentleman wanted to share his brass knuckles with him.

Michael looked at him and said, "I think you should go home. Someone, or something must be waiting for you."

Michael walked away, hoping the young man would not follow him the last block home. He was just a Reservoir Man. Michael got to the apartment, looked back, the van was nowhere in sight. As he walked up the stairs into the living room, Wade was sitting in the dark, but he did not bother Michael, as Wade could tell something was wrong. Wade finally asked him how his night was and if he did well.

Michael said, "I descended into chaos and the depths of the unsavory people. They were lost and somehow needed me to complete their need."

Michael's apartment was a block from Prospect Park. Michael would often go there and sit on the bench for hours, thinking. Michael would occasionally talk to himself; sometimes he mumbled. At times, strangers sat next to him for an intimate encounter or to beg for money to buy liquor. Several of them would join in the conversation without knowing what he was saying.

Michael would just stare at them, give them money, or a smile with a nice, "No thanks."

Michael listened and considered some advice from a friend of Wade's. There was an organization, he told Michael, started by Barnard Haldane that helped individuals transfer from one industry to another on the executive level. The program was a thousand dollars, he told Andy, who gleefully helped him. Andy wanted Michael to leave the entertainment industry.

Michael started the classes and quickly understood Haldane's process of contact referral. You ask someone for a meeting, they meet with you, and you ask them for any contacts that they know that might help you. This contact gives you other contacts, and you ask the new contacts for help—and so on, it multiplies. Michael was serious about this and wanted to give it a chance.

Michael sat in the larger of their two living rooms as he began compiling names. He had about fifteen that held established positions in corporations. He wrote a direct and informative letter to all fifteen asking for help in his quest. He also attached a resume. Now, the wait was on to see if anyone would answer him.

In two weeks, he got six answers to help him, and the others would either keep his resume on file or could not see him. His first meeting was with the President of Western Union. His meeting went well, and the gentleman gave him two additional names to help. The other five meetings went well. Two of the men wanted to talk about their careers, not addressing Michael's need.

Michael received a call from AT&T, who had just wrapped up their lawsuit. The result of the lawsuit was monumental, as it broke AT&T into five smaller companies. The job specs were to develop a central arts policy lasting for at least ten years for all the new smaller companies. Michael had a meeting with a couple of Assistant Vice Presidents and the Vice President for Operations. They told him they needed a few weeks so they could

properly develop their goals. This looked ~~very~~
promising.

Michael also got a call from Gary, the president of
a small company, and he set up ~~the~~ an appointment.
~~His name was~~ Gary, ~~and he~~ had hundreds of
pictures of his two children and his wife. He and
Michael really hit it off, but Michael started to pick up a
strange vibe from him. ~~He~~ Gary asked Michael to dinner
that night, and Michael liked Gary so much that he
accepted. They had a ~~great~~ dinner, laughed, and
talked about the theatre and business in general.
As they were on dessert, Michael boldly asked him
if he was looking for a little more out of the
evening.

Gary directly said "Yes, but now that we
broke the ice, I'd rather have you as a friend."

Michael shook his hand, relieved and
happy. He became Michael's confidant for at least
six years, and they met for dinner once a month.
Michael knew he was a Reservoir Man. But after all
this time, he'd finally met a Reservoir Man who
was honest with himself.

Michael got the job at AT&T. He started and
was excited. He realized how powerful this

company was. They could control all communication in America. He made that statement to several people, including lower-level executives, but they did not respond. Michael was coordinating several projects for them. He would get calls from acquaintances asking for theatre advice. Michael helped them without questioning them. The only problem was that these calls were monitored by AT&T. ~~He missed the theatre~~. The staff at the company was becoming more removed, but ~~and~~ Michael did not care. He was not fond of them, as ~~These employees~~ they were too narrow minded. Michael ~~was going~~ went to the gym at 2:30 pm, which was his lunchtime not the company's. Several AVP's came to his desk, telling him lunch was between 12 and 2.

"If you want to go to the gym that is the time," one of them told him sternly.

As the weeks passed, his activities decreased, and they were assumed by people outside of AT&T. Michael was sitting at his desk looking at pencils when his boss came into his office and told him he had an hour to gather his stuff. He handed him a check for $2,000, and the security guards walked him to the front door.

182

Michael was upset because he did not understand why they would fire him.

In truth, he had not yet adapted to their corporate policies, and he was too free for their rigid ~~rigid~~ process. The question Michael had in his mind was why would they hire a creative position to expand their horizons and not expect him to think outside of the box? They could have at least told him why he was so dangerous to their normalcy and thank~~ed~~ him for all his efforts. Michael was told that's how corporations act.

Michael stood on Chambers Street saying, "Wrong choice! Should have just stayed in the arts."

Wade felt terrible for Michael and said, "Look I have two tickets on Austrian Air to London. How about going for two weeks? I can get off from work." ~~Wade told Michael,~~ "We will just go to the theatre every night and maybe even during the day." Michael never knew Wade paid for the tickets himself. ~~He thought Michael really needed a break.~~

They found an inexpensive Bed & Breakfast on Edgeware Road in London. The trip was cheap, and tailor made for Michael's needs. In Michael's first trip to Europe, he did not make it to London, but now, staying for a few weeks he made up for that earlier loss. They saw twelve plays; they even made their way to Strafford on The Avon. Michael enjoyed going into the Pubs, and he made a lot of friends. London did not have great food, but Michael did learn to like Indian food. He had a wonderful time but was fonder of Paris.

Michael was well rested and about to take on a new adventure. He incorporated his new company, a talent agency. He completed his long-term business plan and looked for office space. He wanted to stay in the Mid-Town area around Broadway. But before he could become serious, he needed to have money. Andy might just be tapped out, not of cash, but of hearing Michael's pitches.

Andy suggested asking his brother-in-law, Brian, who had just divorced his sister. Michael thought he might be a viable candidate, so he took Brian out for dinner with this proposal.

184

Michael told him, "Give me ten thousand dollars, and I will buy a CD with the money."

He wanted the CD to build credit. What he did not tell either his brother-in-law or Andy was that he took the CD to Marine Midland Bank and borrowed nine thousand dollars against the CD. He now had the capital to start the business without touching Brian's money.

Michael looked at ~~so~~ many offices. He really liked a two-room office at 1501 Broadway. It had a ~~this~~ balcony overlooking Times Square and was only $750 per month. What a find! ~~It was sad that no one in his family offered to help~~. Michael set up the office, and he knew that if all else failed, Andy would be there to help him. Everyone in his family was silent except his older sister who bought the rugs, tiles, and designed a beautiful floor.

Michael hired an assistant who worked for free for a while. The deal was that Michael had to submit her boyfriend for acting work. That ~~worked.~~ lasted for about a month. When the boyfriend did not become a star, she left. Michael then hired a young woman who worked for him as an intern in Dover. She was ~~great~~ good and had money, so Michael did not have to pay her in a hurry. She also gave him a little security that he had in Dover.

Even with all the actors he had hired over the years at Dover, not a single agent would give him advice. He was in the dark to all the pitfalls of being an agent. None of the actors he hired in Dover asked Michael to represent them even though some did not have an agent. So, this was all new to him and no lessons in agenting 101. He was on his own.

Michael very slowly began making business friends with some casting directors. One casting director Michael the befriended had a large company and casted most of the Broadway Musicals. They were in the same office building as Michael, and he would go upstairs and visit. Tanner, one of the owners of the casting company, liked Michael very much, and this professional friendship became the root of Michael's success.

Suddenly, Michael's brother-in-law wanted his money back. Michael did not have the money to pay the loan to the bank or any reserve. He cashed in the CD and gave the money back to Brian. The bank called in the loan for the $9,000, as there was

186

no security behind the loan any longer. Michael held the bank off and went to Andy and told him what he did. Andy was so impressed with his business smarts he paid off the $9,000 loan.

Michael was introduced to a wealthy couple from Arizona. Their conversations over dinner were about a play they optioned, and with ~~a great~~ _the right_ cast, it could be a hit. The name of the play was "Moose Murders," and they wanted to cast it with all stars. ~~Michael thought Tanner would like to cast~~ it. He brought it up to Tanner who wanted to do something with Michael. Tanner read the script and met with the couple, ~~And it was~~ a deal. Tanner _and they made_ and his company would cast the play. Due to the rapid growth of the agency, Michael never found the time to read the script and relied on the treatment.

The producer's money was getting thin. The couple went from casting stars to just good actors. The script was not good, but with lots of stars, it could have been fun. However, they could not afford them. Tanner had a tough time dealing with the production staff. Michael begged out because of all the arguing going on. Tanner was not happy but in all his kindness laughed it off.

187

The production had a lot of trouble with the cast coming and going. Finally, the play opened to some of the worst reviews in the history of Broadway. Michael was happy he had left. Tanner was not as happy about casting the worst production in Broadway history, but for a long time, they laughed about this adventure.

Tanner would occasionally ask Michael to drive him to Allentown, Pennsylvania, to see a pre-Broadway Musical that Tanner's office cast. Michael enjoyed the company, so two hours one way with Tanner was fun. Coming back, there were a few cast members that Michael drove back to New York at Tanner's request. They were chorus members who had an opinion on everything. Michael prevailed and laughed at times, but it was a little tense driving.

At the end of the run, they sent to Michael's office a large basket of fruit. Michael thought this must have some subtextual meaning but was grateful. Michael's business was taking off, and he was making money. He often thought of Ben and how he missed him, but he was happy he did not take him on this crazy financial ride. He still had not called him, as he was so afraid to hear he might not be doing well. He wanted to ~~say sorry~~, but how do you _apologize_ say sorry to someone you might have hurt? Sorry was not the right word, but what was?

Wade came home with serious news, saying that his company was moving to Connecticut in the next few months. Wade did not know what to do. They discussed Wade commuting, but it would take too long. Wade offered a suggestion: why not move to Connecticut? His company would find an apartment and give them the security deposit and pay for the moving. Michael was thinking even further. He would get his security deposit back and his first month rent from the Park Slope apartment, ~~which he could really use.~~

Michael could either commute or stay in the city at a friend's apartment who was out of town for six months. Michael decided he would stay at the friend's apartment and commute to the city when he stayed in Connecticut. Wade asked Michael if he could meet an old Navy friend that was looking for advice. Michael asked what kind of advice.

Wade said, "He wants to get out of the military. A friend was killed working next to him on their submarine when a huge girder fell on top of him."

Michael said without hesitation, "Sure, have him come over before we move." Wade's friend came over the next night.

Bobby, Wade's friend, was early by two hours, but it was a small gathering of three. Michael could not keep his eyes off Bobby. He was like "Billy Budd" with all the features Melville described. Wade saw this connection between Michael and Bobby and became very uneasy. Michael spent a few hours talking to him, telling him what procedures and actions to take without having any derogatory mentions on his discharge papers. Bobby was ready to go. It was going to be extremely hard to convince his commanding officer, but Bobby was going to try.

Wade secured an apartment in Bethel, Connecticut; Michael came up and checked out the city. Bethel which was a charming small village. Michael loved the apartment; it was perfect for the dogs, which were now two. He bought a Jeep with the return of his security deposit from the Park Slope apartment and a trade in of his car, which was more than enough for a large deposit on the Jeep. Michael stayed back waiting for the movers, and Wade stayed at a hotel that his new company paid, ~~for~~ for.

All was perfect. Michael was sitting in his Brooklyn apartment with no TV. ~~The phone~~ and no phone. ~~company turned off the phone two days too early.~~ The movers would be there in thirty-six hours. Suddenly, the doorbell rang. Michael ~~thought to~~ wondered ~~himself~~ how it could ~~not~~ be the movers at 7 pm. He went downstairs and opened the door only to see Bobby. The Naval base had started the paperwork, and he would be out in a month. Michael could not believe how quick it all happened. ~~Bobby said he~~ To celebrate, ~~was persistent.~~ Michael ran out and bought a bottle of wine. They drank and laughed all night and then had breakfast together.

Bobby left with Michael and the movers. When they got to the Connecticut apartment, Wade seemed a bit put off. He was extremely cold to Bobby, so much so, that Wade asked Michael to take Bobby home or to the train. Michael said he would drive him into the city since he forgot something at the office. They got to the city and

191

Michael went directly to his sublet with Bobby, where they stayed for a few days.

Michael told Wade he was going to stay in the city because he had a few problems in the office. Michael went back to Connecticut that weekend. He asked Wade what his problem was with Bobby. Wade said he did not intend for Michael to get that friendly with Bobby. Michael was confused.

"We are not in a relationship, what difference would it make?"

"Plenty," said Wade. "We built a home over all these years, and now, there is three."

Michel grabbed Wade and said, "Sure, there is a relationship, but it was a friendship. I never gave you any idea it was more."

Wade said, "You are right. I am sorry for making this difficult. Let's have a Cape Cod." They both laughed.

As time passed, Wade met a friend who he really connected with, and it became a strong relationship. Michael decided it would be better to stay in the city. He found ~~this great~~ apartment on

West 47th Street, a duplex in Hell's Kitchen. He called Wade about getting his furniture.

Wade said, "Take your personal things. Everything else is mine!" Michael got angry and told him this was not true.

Wade said, "It is true! You owe this to me. All the favors I did for you."

Michael forcibly said, "I paid you back, buddy, and helped you all those years in Dover and Georgia." Michael accepted his irrational arguments rather than have an ugly situation.

Michael said, "Fine, I want to come into the apartment without you there. Have the dogs ready for me."

Wade wanted one of the dogs and Michael knew this was his new friend's idea. Michael told Wade, "Those dogs are mine. They carry my emotions and history."

Michael moved into his new apartment, only to find a dead man leaning against his window, outside on the ground floor of his duplex. The gentrification of Hell's Kitchen was far from complete. In the middle of all this, Michael took on

193

a partner, Ross. The office was growing, and he needed someone to share the responsibilities. Both Ross and Michael agreed that they would have to bring in another agent to share more of the workload.

Michael was smoking heavily but enjoyed every moment he held a cigarette in his mouth or fingers. Two of Michael's musical theatre clients invited him to a reading of "Life is not a Doris Day Movie." The plot was about four gas station attendants who become transported to Oz. One actor assumed the identity of the Lion, another the Tinman, another Scarecrow, and the last was Dorothy. The libretto was all the contemporary music, and it was fun.

Michael got involved. He called a friend from his MFA program, Dean, who had just partnered with a prominent General Manager named May. They hired them to act as General Managers. They secured the Village Gate, a good venue for a musical. A gentleman from a fledgling company, Showtime, in its initial stages, wanted to start shooting small off-Broadway Musicals and air them after the shows closed. The gentleman hung around with the group until the show opened.

Though the audience enjoyed the show, the reviews were horrible. The morning after opening was painful for the cast and creators, and the man from Showtime was nowhere to be found. Dean and his partner did not want to be paid for the wrap up of the box office or front of the house business.

About a month after the show closed, Michael got a call from May telling him that Dean, Michael's Manager for "Life is not a Doris Day Movie" had passed away. The wake would be in The Village. May was really upset, and Michael never got the reason from her how Dean died.

Michael went to the wake with tons of flowers and mass cards. ~~Michael bought a perpetual mass card~~. No one from school was there. Dean was close to Eliott, the Dean of the MFA program. Michael was extremely nervous ~~not about to run~~ running into him. If he came, Michael would be nice but firm. Michael asked one of Dean's family members if anyone came from the school. He was told no, but many of Dean's local friends were there to support the family.

The funeral home was in the neighborhood where Dean grew up in the West Village. His sister came up to Michael, thanking him for coming. Michael now had the opportunity to ask how Dean ~~had~~ had died.

The sister said, "Amoebas. He must have picked them up at Fire Island a few months ago. It had to be in the water or something. The doctors could not cure him, and his death was not nice."

Michael could not understand why no one came from their school; Dean was not loved, but he was respected. Dean died from something rare, and his death confused Michael.

Michael was having a tough time with his new ~~brought on~~ partner, Ross. Ross had worked with a middle-sized agency, which gave him a ~~excellent~~ good foundation in the industry. The problem with Ross was that he would repeat everything Michael said and sat at his desk pulling at his cheek nonstop. This image and action were very disconcerting to Michael. Michael could not get over the fact that Ross would repeat everything Michael said as if the idea ~~was~~ were his own. Ross ~~did have~~ had a good relationship with the clients, and he was well read, which meant a lot to Michael. He was amazed how many younger agents had no literary knowledge before the 20th century. What really bothered Michael the most was that when he would have a discussion with Ross, it was like talking to himself, ~~he never took an administrative position which was hard to deal with~~. There was too much going on around Michael for him to focus on Ross's communication problems.

They started to interview new potential agents. They liked this one candidate who worked as an assistant to an agent in a large talent agency, Gail. They agreed to hire her, and Michael and Gail became friends. Gail was ~~very~~ jovial, chubby, and short. She had a broad southern accent and short blonde hair. Gail also had a small scar on her cheek. Michael thought this was a sign that she will work out, like his lip she also had a scar. Gail was forever on diets and diet soda. Michael and Gail would love to go after work to an upscale Thai restaurant that had a great happy hour. Michael drank his vodka straight with water as a chaser. No more Cape Cods.

Michael and Gail became close. Gail, on several occasions, would go home to Michael's parents for some great Italian cooking. Gail became a good agent, but Michael noticed she had a similar problem as Ross. She repeated all the opinions of Michael as if she never had an original thought about the industry. ~~This was a relationship blessed by God but created somewhere else.~~

To get away from it all, Michael found solace on a unique bench across the street from the office. The messages on the bench were the best etched ever. The bench spoke of many sad people who lost a love there. Other etchings captured pure happiness. All these messages were carved ~~with a knife~~ into the bench. When Michael sat on the bench, he felt all these people were there with him. He felt their pain and understood them, sometimes more than the people who were around him.

Bobby met Michael at work to go to dinner and a play. Michael did not want to eat; he would rather sit on his bench until curtain time. Bobby came and sat next to him on the bench. Michael looked up and saw Mark walking down the street toward them with yet another new dog. Michael reminded him that he could not take on any new dogs. They all laughed. Mark had just completed his MFA program in acting from Yale. Michael was so happy for him. Mark asked if he could be represented by Michael's office.

"Sure, come up next week, and we will set you up," said Michael.

Mark looked satisfied, but the moment passed, and his face turned to stone. Mark asked Michael if he heard about this new gay cancer going around.

Michael responded, "How can a cancer be gay?" It did not make any sense.

"My friend has the gay cancer. He has all these marks on his back and face. He said he has fevers, and he is not eating," said Mark.

Michael tried to reassure him but was not sure what to say. Mark said good night and left them. Michael suddenly did not want to go to the theatre.

He sat on the bench saying, "Could you imagine a gay cancer?"

CHAPTER FOURTEEN

1983-1988

Michael's problems with Ross became much more critical. Ross was advising clients with no collaboration from Michael or even Gail. Michael now believed this short partnership needed to end. Michael and Gail devised a plan that they would both go into partnership.

Gail produced the execution plan. Michael would tell Ross that he was thinking about retiring, and he had his fill of the industry. Gail would come in with $15,000 from her mother, enough to float the office for at least two months. Gail would secure new office space and change the name of the company and file for a new corporation. They would deal with the unions and the city after they were in the office operating. Then At the end of the week, the clients would be told of the move.

Michael remained in the office working with Ross while Gail was out doing all the elements of starting a new office. They would meet in their favorite Thai restaurant every night.

The startup took ten days before they were ready to go. Michael and Gail spoke to all the clients over the weekend and informed them that they did not owe commissions to anyone since Michael's name was on their contract with the old agency. They would move their employment contracts to their new agency. All of clients approved of this action. On Monday morning, Ross sat in the empty office not yet knowing what happened. He started to call clients and they informed him that they were with the new agency. Confused, he called around to verify this news, only to discover he had no clients. But he did have an office since his name was on the lease as well as Michael's.

Ross's father called Michael and did not have fond words for Michael's actions. There was nothing that Ross could do. He was checkmated. Michael and Gail were on a quest to build a strong and influential agency. Michael did feel bad for Ross; all Michael wanted to do was to service his clients with passion and truth, developing their career even if the payoff took a while.

It seemed ~~that so~~ many people in the industry supported their move. They began drawing a small salary three weeks after opening. Michael was able to get the license from the city and the franchises from the two unions, SAG and AEA. They hired an assistant for the office. She was good ~~great~~, but she left after four weeks. She had had problems with Gail. The second new assistant was male and a true "Yes" man. ~~He and Gail we~~re ~~simply fine now.~~ Michael was also garnishing a reputation in the industry for having an incredible eye for talent, as demonstrated in a growing list of new actors and ~~best~~ clients.

had — Michael and Gail represented ~~a great~~ an actor who just landed the replacement for the lead in a major Broadway show. During rehearsals, the actor became extremely sick and developed pneumonia. It was told to Michael that he was HIV positive and had developed several conditions related to AIDS. He was also contracted to do a small ~~but nice~~ role in a film. He got out of the hospital and had to resign the from play, performing the play would be too stressful and dangerous in his condition. He did

202

report to the set for the film, but they had heard he had AIDS. The producers came into the dressing room to help put on his makeup and he finished his scene. He died four-weeks after this incident at the age of forty-five years old. Michael was devastated. He genuinely liked and respected this actor, whose personal dignity was saved by the actions of the film producers. Michael wondered how long this disease would go on, how many people it would touch, and he was afraid.

Gail became very pushy and nasty. Within a month after they began operation of the company, Gail wanted her mother to be paid back the $15,000. This would be extremely hard, and an increase in salary for both Gail and Michael seemed dim. Michael tried to make her understand that this request was going to be painful for all concerned, but she would not listen. He wondered if this meant that Gail and her mother did not believe the company would survive.

Michael was drinking again—one step below drinking heavily. He went back to seeking anonymous encounters due to the stress of the agency and this new virus outbreak. These encounters created a problem because some contacts would find out where he lived and stand outside the house calling his name endlessly. It was very embarrassing. One night when he had a few clients at the house for drinks, Richard stood outside for an hour calling his name and knocking on the door. Michael quickly ended his nightly excursions.

Michael would go to his parents' house every Sunday for Macaroni dinner. Even if he stayed for only a half an hour, he would drive about an hour to be with his parents and macaroni. Andy would always walk him to his car, getting a chance to talk to Michael. Their discussions would vary from economics to politics.

On this Sunday, Andy got profoundly serious. He told Michael he had some health issues. He jumped over a three-foot fence and fell. This happened about two months ago. About two months ago, he had He went to his doctor who referred him to a specialist. After a series of tests, the doctor had discovered the reappearance of the tumor on his kidney. During the operation, a small malignant cell fell off, which appeared to have affected his lung and his bones.

This malignant cell started to spread through ~~out~~ **rapidly** Andy's body, ~~rapidly~~.

~~Michael felt as if he was cut in half—one half of him was Andy, who he was going to lose.~~ Andy assured him that the doctors seemed positive **about** ~~for~~ his future treatments. Michael went back to his apartment; Bobby took Michael out for a few drinks. Michael called his sister. She told him it was bad, Frances did not know the extent of the illness, but Andy remained positive.

As the weeks passed, Andy took a turn for the worse. He was in terrible pain; ~~Michael would go into the office at 6 am, do his work, and leave at 8 am. He would then walk a mile to pick up his Jeep to drive to Brooklyn.~~ **Michael began shortening his work day.** The only thing Frances did was cook; her kitchen was **always** full of ~~a~~ multitude of Italian aromas. Within a week, she cooked every dish that Andy loved, but he barely ate anything. Still, she continued to cook. Michael built a bond with his younger sister while being together every day with one objective, making Andy comfortable.

Bobby was incredibly supportive of Michael as well as many of Michael's clients. Andy's journey became increasingly more difficult as he struggled

to hold on. Andy ~~loved living~~ *lived* more as an observer
than someone who was proactive. For a man who
had only a third-grade education, he was about to
leave his children over a million dollars and provide
for Frances with an additional trust.

Andy was a superman ~~of~~ *for* those who knew
him and his achievements. It was always his family
first. Michael did not know what he would do when
Andy was gone. He must take care of Frances, that
was one thing he knew for sure. His lifestyle both
at work and at leisure were going to make it
extremely hard. There was no way he would ever
abandon Frances; she would just have to come
along wherever he was.

Andy's journey toward death started to
make startling new twists. Andy started calling *out*
dead people's names repeatedly at times, asking
them to take him away. He would tell Frances to
get his coffin, he was ready. Frances was terrified,
especially the night she was alone and mysteriously
got locked into her bedroom. She was unable to
get out of the room, and Andy was alone in the
living room. She was on the floor all night in her
bedroom crying. As these incidents grew in one

direction or another, Andy got worse, closer to death.

On a rainy night in August, his night attendant was sitting next to Andy when suddenly he was thrown to the floor, and it felt as if he was being kicked repeatedly. He ran from the house screaming. Frances was just stunned. At his car, he called Michael's sister. He told her he would not go back, and that the devil was in Andy's room. Andy became still the next few days; the family was able to talk to him individually. Michael came up to the bed and thanked him for the wonderful life he shared with him. Michael told his father that he was content with all the life choices he personally had made. Andy weakly held Michael's hand.

The next night, a hurricane hit New York. Andy began moaning again but now just calling one name, John. Though the family knew a lot of Johns, Frances's brother was the most likely. John died while in the Navy. Andy's calling of John was different than the others, as if he felt him near and was trying to reach out to him. This continued for hours. Andy died at 8:30 am on John's birthday.

Stuck in the Brooklyn Battery Tunnel, Michael missed saying his final goodbye to his father.

~~Michael was stuck in the Brooklyn Battery Tunnel for 45 minutes. He missed saying the final goodbye to Andy~~. When he came up the elevator, his brother-in-law Carl, was waiting. He attempted to console him. Michael was polite but wanted ~~no part of it, he wanted~~ only to see Andy. Michael walked into the apartment and saw ~~Andy~~ his father on the bed with a towel wrapped around his chin to close his mouth. It was not Andy anymore. Michael just looked at his shell, a sight ~~Michael~~ he would experience repeatedly throughout his life.

As he stood there, the undertaker ~~came~~ arrived. ~~They put something or someone else in a body bag, but it was not Andy.~~ Since the family was very friendly with the ~~funeral home~~ people at the funeral home, they knew personally how Andy did not want to be embalmed. ~~Andy~~ He was taken to the funeral home and placed on ice until all family and friends could be notified. ~~Andy~~ His body was shown for only one day and one night. The funeral home was packed~~, and~~ it took three funeral parlor rooms to house the family, friends, and ~~the~~ flowers. It was an incredible night. Frances wore a black veil, and when you looked at her, she was radiant. She almost looked like a young bride but with a black veil not a white one over her face. Michael's young nephew came over to him and asked why he was not crying, like his own mother and father were.

Michael smiled gently and said, "Men do not cry, but I hurt more than ever. Oh God, do I hurt."

The funeral procession to the church was a sight. ~~Andy was very friendly with the people around the shop~~. As they passed the shop and the streets following, there were people standing in front of their homes waving at the hearse. Andy was close with the minority residents around the shop, and they too came to wave goodbye.

At the church, several of Michael's musical theatre clients sang some of Andy's favorite songs. The mass was celebrated in Italian. At the cemetery, those that came walked to the gravesite. The Knights of Columbus and Michael's younger sister organized a great buffet for the family and friends. There was a stillness amongst the crowd, but a lot of warmth among all those that came. This would be the first night Frances would be without ~~Andy~~ her husband, but all three children stayed in the living room all night making sure she was fine. Michael was lost; he felt so empty.

Michael went right back to work. Every other day he would visit ~~Frances~~ his mother. Michael began having strange dreams; the images were very faint. It was a party at a beach house, but he did not know any one at this party. This dream ~~was~~ recurred ~~recurring~~ every night for about two weeks. What was even stranger was that as he approached the end of the second week, the images of the beach house became more defined, as did the faces of the nameless guests. He did not discuss his dreams with anyone, preferring to forget them.

Michael spent the next few months grieving and working. His drinking and smoking got worse, and he developed a bad cough. He went to the doctors and found ~~to find~~ out he had bronchitis. Michael had a female friend and client, Judy, who ~~really~~ cared for him. She moved upstairs in his apartment house. He always came home to a meal Judy cooked, and ~~which~~ all three of them ate together every night, Michael, Judy, and Bobby. Michael had produced a revival of her cabaret show. Judy used to be a big cabaret name who then fell on tough times.

Norman Lear did a show called "The Judith Cohen Story" on "Good Times," and the whole episode was about her. But Judy was humble about her fate and incredibly happy to know Michael. Bobby got an excellent job at an upscale Mexican restaurant and was bringing in a good salary. Events around Michael seemed good, but his heart was still heavy with the loss of his father. Most people loved and admired Andy, but nobody loved and admired him like Michael.

Michaels's office was working with several Los Angles affiliate talent agencies. One agency was owned by a guy who had two excellent agents and an assistant working in his office. Michael's office only shared one client with this office, and the actor had a lead on a show with MGM. This LA affiliate took care of him; the client was incredibly happy to work with them.

One day, Michael got a call from one of the girls who said the owner had not been in the office for three weeks. There was no answer at his home. Michael suggested she wait a little longer. Two weeks came and still no answer. The girls had not been paid in five weeks. Michael thought the owner was in financial trouble, and he just dropped out of sight for whatever reason. He told them to ask the management of the building if he owed back rent, which they found out he did not. They checked with the other vendors he used, and everything was fine. All his bills had been paid.

They asked Michael if he would take over his office. Michael was reluctant but told the girls he would think it over.

He went into Gail's office, and she quickly told him, "Don't look at me for any money." Michael explained to her what a great chance this would be.

"It would save us a lot in startup operating capital if we had to open completely on our own in LA. Taking over this office would save us a considerable amount of money."

Gail's response was still negative and told him if he wanted to do it, it was fine—but she would not put any money into the venture. At this point, he questioned if Gail should have stayed an employee rather than an owner. She proved not to be a risk taker. Feeling confused with Gail's reaction, he did not know what to do. Suddenly, his assistant called on the intercom saying there was a man on the phone calling himself Ben from Dover.

Michael jumped on the phone saying, "Ben, it is so great to hear from you!"

Ben, sounding firm, said, "The same here, how is your health?"

Michael said, "Great!"

Ben said quickly. "Are you HIV positive?"

"No," Michael said.

He then heard a click, and Ben was gone. Michael wondered how many guys were making similar calls to former friends. Michael was still hoping that one day he would be able to say sorry to Ben.

Michael made several calls to LA, especially to regulatory State agencies in California, who regulate theatrical agencies, and it seemed what he was proposing in taking over the office was possible. He called the management company of the building who told him once he officially took over the company, they would use the prior owner's security deposit to pay any back rent and send any balance to his home. Michael would have to put his own security deposit down.

The union told him the clients would have to break their current contracts and sign separately with his company. Michael took some of his inheritance from his father—about $60,000—as the initial seed money. Before he formalized the new company, he flew to LA to meet the staff and check the place out.

He stayed at the Highland Gardens, where he had stayed when he came to LA to see two of his clients in the National Company of "Amadeus." This hotel would not be the first choice of anyone coming to LA because of its history. Janis Joplin died of an overdose there. ~~Many people believed she still haunted the hotel.~~ Guests who stayed at the hotel maintained that room 105, where she died, was haunted. Michael loved the hotel with all the overgrown plants on the hotel property. It was funky. It remined him of his set for "Suddenly Last Summer" at Dover. The thought of Dover always gave Michael comfort.

When Michael arrived in LA, Debbie, the office assistant, met him at the airport and took him directly to the office. The staff of three took him to dinner and spent a lot of time with him. Michael rented a car but got lost driving after his long dinner. He finally found the hotel, checked in, went to his room, and collapsed. The next day, he met with the building management and the union; all went well.

Emma, one of the two agents in the office, was a good agent and a nice person. She took Michael to two apartments she knew about in Playa Del Rey as Michael wanted a place near the beach. They found the perfect apartment overlooking the ocean. Emma lived in Playa Del Rey, which made it more tempting for Michael because he could live near someone he knew.

Michael had to make the hard decision to stay or return to New York. He spent the next day on the phone with Bobby, Gail, and his family, especially his mother. Everyone seemed supportive, though he told Frances that he was going for only six months then come home. This was true since Michael was not going to commit to living permanently in LA.

Michael liked what he saw from both a business ~~prospective~~ perspective as well as a personal viewpoint. He told the LA staff he was going to take the apartment at the beach and be back in three weeks. He knew he had to drive back with his jeep. He was not going to miss this opportunity; these girls had a great business foundation, something that would have taken a long time to develop, in addition to a ~~great~~ LA client list. ~~And everyone was nice.~~ good

Before Michael left for New York to plan for his six months' stay in LA, he went back to the apartment at the beach to check it out one more time. He found a park bench right outside of the apartment facing the canal leading from the marina to the ocean. He realized a large reason he so easily agreed to leave New York was that he had ~~lost so~~ many friends in a horrific and brief amount of time.

There was Lenny, the young man who wore his mother's wig and house dress. His two Central Park friends Eliott and Jerry ~~who~~ had died a week apart. His stage manager in Dover, Barry. Bruce, an intern at Dover. Ramon, a close friend who was a successful Spanish director. Dean, a good business associate and a college buddy. How could this happen to

216

such good, young people? Just taken for no reason other than they wanted to love.

Michael began seeing some of his friends who had died walking on the street in Manhattan. He held himself back, knowing that it was not them. ~~Michael wished that the friends he saw were real.~~ On two occasions without thinking, he approached one of these dead friends to say 'hello,' but he was ~~very~~ embarrassed that they were someone else. He wondered if he was the only guy in New York to have this happen. But then he read in the newspaper about the mirage of those that passed and how they were still seen walking the streets by family and friends.

Michael came home, Bobby was under the impression they were both moving to LA. Michael said that it was not true.

"I am going for six months then coming home. You are always able to visit if you can get the time off from work."

The next day he went into the office and told Gail his plan for opening the LA office, that he would use his father's money. Michael told ~~Gail~~ her he would come back to New York after six months.

stay in LA. ~~and~~ She ~~aggressively said to~~ advised him that if
he ~~is~~ was not at the office full time, those girls ~~will~~ would steal
the office from them.

He said, "If that was the case, why did they
not just start their own office when their boss
left?"

Obviously, Gail wanted the playing field to
herself in New York. Michael told her that if he
could get Frances out to LA, he might consider
staying ~~in LA~~ there.

Her last words to Michael at the end of the
meeting were, "You'll be sorry if you don't move
there."

Bobby got ready for Michael's departure.
Michael felt like he was a new unwritten character
in Jack Kerouac's "On the Road." He even took the
book with him. His last night in New York was spent
with Frances, ~~having her great sauce.~~ She made
spaghetti and peas in a light marinara sauce for dinner.

The next morning, he got into his car, ready
for his new adventure. He did not realize yet that
Hollywood was on the verge of a writers' strike
that might last a ~~very~~ long time and that would

stop all productions in the country. What he also did not know as he pulled away from his house, was that he had already lost twenty-nine friends or business acquaintances to AIDS.

CHAPTER FIFTEEN

1989-1991

Michael driving alone was very peaceful for his condition, and well-being. Michael always talked about the beauty of European architecture; it was the history and the people who embodied their culture demonstrated by their art. Michael realized that the beauty of America was just as great, if not greater than Europe's Europe had the history, America the majesty of the mountains and the plains. He found the towns in Louisiana, Texas, and especially New Mexico so friendly and welcoming, Michael decided to slow down and enjoy America.

Michael found a bench in the White Desert in New Mexico. He was amazed at the calm and purity that surrounded him while he sat for hours. He thought of all the friends who died and pictured all the great times he had with them. He thought of

Andy, of what a good man he was and how no matter what problems Michael got into, ~~Andy~~ His father forgave and understood. Michael felt cleansed and at peace going into LA as he continued to think of ~~Andy and Frances.~~ his parents.

Michael arrived in LA at 5:30 pm ~~going~~ and went directly to his apartment. He parked the car, got his bags, dropped them off, and went to sit on the bench outside his apartment. He saw the sunset, and it was incredible. He thought about how beautiful it was to see this every night while living at the beach. The California sunsets collapsed into the sky taking with it the smallness of the remaining rays of the sun. Then twilight produced an amber glow on surroundings hills. This vision was just the beginning of Michael's appreciation for the fantastic beauty that existed in and out of Los Angles. Michael clamored for the chance to see it all.

The writers officially went on strike a few days after Michael's arrival. The staff were genuinely concerned why it took Michael so long to make his journey.

Michael simply said, "I didn't want to miss all those great vistas that made New Mexico and Arizona special."

During his initial stay Michael got to know the new LA clients, made a few friends—one was Richard, whose companion was a casting director. Michael and Richard had so much simpatico. They spent hours talking when Richard came up to the office to visit. Richard taught Michael the lay of the land in Hollywood. while Michael asked Richard on numerous occasions to have a drink, Richard always declined. Richard did observe that Michael really enjoyed his Vodka Martini.

Michael retorted, "I do not drink at home. You could not find a bottle in my house." This was Michael's chant that he was not an alcoholic, only a social drinker.

Michael and Richard's friendship took a negative turn. Michael was unaware that Richard's best friend did not know that Richard was HIV positive. Richard only told Michael and his family, Michael inadvertently alluded to this to Richard's friend, who panicked and went back to Richard with this knowledge. Richard stopped talking to Michael. ~~Richard progressively got worse,~~

The staff used this time to set up general meetings for the actors to meet casting directors. Michael got requests from several of his high-profile actors in the New York Office to come to Hollywood. Michael welcomed them. Some of these clients even asked if they could stay with him.

"Sure, I am lonely," said Michael.

This gave Michael the chance to bond with them and to have more than a minute of conversation about their residency and career in Hollywood and what work might be available. Michael got used to sleeping on the couch, giving the actor his bedroom.

He had a strange incident. One of his high-profile actors who stayed with him insisted he sleep in the bed with him and not have Michael sleep on the couch. Michael did not know what to say other than, "No." This posed a problem ~~of~~ with Michael rejecting him. It also put a strain on their friendship. The relationship was healed, if it ever needed to be, when Michael invited both him and his wife to stay in his new home in Beverley Hills. They stayed for five weeks while looking for an apartment. Michael had a friend in New York, Troy, who asked if he could visit.

Michael said, "Sure."

The night Troy arrived, he took a cab from the airport and rang Michael's doorbell; Michael came to the door to see his ~~beautiful~~ friend standing there with a small suitcase. Troy weighed no more than one hundred pounds.

Michael grabbed his friend and hugged him, saying, "How great for you to be ~~with me.~~ here."

Michael enjoyed showing him ~~all of~~ around Hollywood. They both took in the legendary sunsets on the bench outside his apartment and discussed events happening in their lives. Troy explained to Michael ~~he contracted~~ that he had HIV first, but it rapidly turned ~~in to~~ into AIDS. Troy had Kaposi Sarcoma. He took off his shirt, and Michael was truly horrified with all the markings on his body. ~~Troy said it was an honor to be with him. He~~ Troy went on to explain that it was so rare to be treated not as an outcast but as a welcomed friend. He told Michael the doctors said he only had a few months to ~~go.~~ live.

224

While Troy enjoyed seeing LA with his friend, Michael.
Michael reflected on how hard it must have been
on those parents to look at their child wasting
away at twenty-one or twenty-two years old. The
child that they barely how out on the road to life. He
understood why some of these parents just left in
horror and flew back to their homes before their
child died. Michael drove Troy to the airport. On the end of Troy's visit, At the
gate, they hugged and said goodbye, knowing it
was their last goodbye.

Troy said, "I will be saying a lot of goodbyes
in the coming months but none as meaningful as
this goodbye to my friend, Michael."

Michael decided to stay in LA, but he had to
fly back to New York to make plans to move his
furnishings to LA. He did not want to leave the
sunsets, the deserts, mountains, and the grandeur.
He and Emma set out to find him a permanent
apartment in LA, which they did within two days.
There was still this doubt in Michael's emotions
about moving to LA, mainly because of Frances his mother.
Deciding to drive rather than fly,
Michael got into his Jeep the next morning,
driving back to New York. He decided to drive and
not fly. He wanted to celebrate the beauty he saw

on his last trip. Michael's first stop was the desert outside of Needles, California. It had an old-style Western hotel, which was incredibly old and also housed lots of crickets. This posed a problem for Michael. He had never killed an insect in his life, and he was not going to start now. It turned out to be a delightful evening of a large chorus of crickets singing to him.

In New York, Michael met with Gail, telling her he was very torn about leaving New York because of his mother.

Gail hit the roof. "Can't you see those girls in LA will steal the company? Do you trust them if you are not there?"

Michael said, "Yes, they give me no reason to distrust them."

Michael was so mad at Gail's inability to trust. He so wanted to stay in New York because of his mother and to prove to Gail the girls would not harm him or the office. His heart was in New York, and so was his mother. Days passed, and Michael thought about what he should do.

Michael called Gail and said, "I am going to stay in LA because it would not be fair to the LA staff and the LA clients."

What confused Michael was his knowledge that Gail had a good side, but this new personality that she was exhibiting was ~~scary~~ not good for the future of the company. Michael drove up to his apartment in New York to find Judy and Bobby sitting on the porch.

"Where were you?" They said in unison.

"Just seeing a little bit more of America. Have you two been sitting here waiting for me the whole two weeks?"

Judy smiled. "For someone that found so many faults in this country, you sure made a 180-degree turn."

"Once you travel, you'll understand," said Michel with a smile.

Michael was ~~going to drive back to LA~~ glad he had driven his Jeep to New York. He did not want all his valuables in a moving truck or at an airport check in. Bobby was going to fly out after the movers came and finish his last week at the restaurant.

227

Michael went to Brooklyn to spend the day with Frances. There were no misconceptions, and she was sad. Michael gave her brochures of an airline that only the rich and famous took, the MGM Grand. He told her it would be easy now that she was in a wheelchair because these airliners cater to travelers who have a handicap.

"Also, I can get you an apartment on a month-to-month basis near my house," said Michael.

Frances beamed. "You're not making this up, are you?"

"No, it's Los Angles. It's all true," responded Michael.

Michael went home that night only to have one of those damn dreams again, the kind he had right after Andy passed ^his father^. The images were much clearer this time. He did not know a single person in the dream, but he noticed that things in the environment were much different.

Two nights before Michael went back to LA, his apartment was full of well-wishers. Of course, Gail was there saying she did not want Michael to

228

go—what would she do without him? Everyone was excited. Michael was touched by the good will and love he felt from everyone. He spent his last day in New York cleaning the mess from his party. Bobby ordered Chinese food for dinner. Michael had a martini, which Bobby bought at a local bar, because Michael still did not keep liquor in the house.

In the middle of an intense conversation with Bobby, the phone rang. Michael ~~went to answer~~ answered it. It was Eliott, the Dean of his graduate school. Eliott congratulated Michael on all his being ~~success. Michael knew he was~~ the most successful student that graduated in the MFA program.

Eliott asked Michael, "Why are you telling people that I said for you to dig ditches? You misunderstood me, and even if I did say that I was only kidding. I would prefer if we could forget that incident."

Michael said, "That was the most hurtful statement anyone had made to me in my life. You cannot imagine how hurt I felt. You were my mentor, my teacher."

Eliott asked him to accept his apology. Michael went quiet. He sensed something wrong or odd in Eliott's voice.

Michael said, "Yes, I accept, and the incident is forgotten."

Eliott said, "Now, Michael do you love me?"

Michael said, "No, I respect you."

The conversation ended, and they never spoke again.

CHAPTER SIXTEEN

1991-1992

Michael woke up at 5 am, showered, dressed, and left, riding down the West Side highway to the George Washington Bridge on to US 80 West. A few of his friends gave him tapes for the trip, including Piaf, Mina, Brell, and his new love Nina Simone. He was bouncing down the interstate loudly playing his music.

Michael was on to a new beginning. He rushed his cross-country journey, only stopping once for an extended period at the Grand Canyon. He was captivated by the rock formations and the colors of the rocks as he sat on a bench at the Western Rim. Looking down, he saw the Colorado River. It all looked like a post card. He now knew what the Transcendentalists must have felt like in their communion with nature in New England. He understood Whitman, Thoreau, and Emerson so much more.

In Arizona, he got in his Jeep and got back on to I-40 to I-10 and took that directly to Playa Del Rey. He went to his new apartment, which had five levels. ~~All the rooms were on separate levels~~. The apartment was overlooking a small lake only one block from the ocean. He parked in the underground lot, went upstairs, and opened the door to an empty apartment. Michael did not care if the apartment was empty. He was left a sleeping bag, paper plates, cups, and plastic (dinner wear) by his LA staff. Michael, lying in the sleeping bag, **dinnerwa** heard the ocean waves and felt at peace—as at peace as he normally did when sitting on a bench.

Michael spent the next day getting the telephone and utilities up. **hooked** He avoided going into the office. The office staff received a call from the movers that they would arrive in two days. Emma drove over to the apartment to tell him. He thanked her and offered to take her out to dinner. She accepted, they had great Italian food, and afterward, he invited her to watch the sunset with him.

Emma's personality though was of a working-class Bostonian. She was overly sensitive, always chain smoking. Michael sat with her on his bench in front of his old apartment and told her just to watch the sun, to watch the warmth of its beautiful golden glow.

Michael turned to her. "Now watch as it goes down. The earth will eat it up, saving it for the next day."

Emma had tears in her eyes. It was the first time she experienced the sunset this way. Emma and Michael became good friends. Michael, on occasion, would walk on the beach and see Emma sitting on the bench watching the sunset alone.

The furniture came, and Bobby was right behind, landing at LAX. Bobby was impressed by the apartment. They both were so excited that they put the apartment together in two days. The five-month writers' strike was over now, and business was getting back to normal. Their clients began booking jobs, but Michael had a deadline to meet. His business' reserve capital was running near zero. The staff was put back on full salary after six months of partial salary due to the writer's strike.

Michael spoke to Gail, who appeared sympathetic about the lack of capital for the LA office, but she told him she was unable to financially contribute to the company, nor could the New York Office, since they were not doing well. Michael took an additional fifteen thousand dollars from his savings to further underwrite the LA office. Michael had not been paid a full salary for six months, but Andy's money kept him going as he had no income. Bobby landed a wonderful job as an assistant manager at a high-quality restaurant in. Beverly Hills. Things started to come together nicely.

The company had a strong London affiliate. Michael made a few trips to London for business, and he got a chance to get over to Paris for a few days. In addition, Michael booked a client on a TV movie, which was shooting in Paris. The network gave the actor two extra first-class tickets. The client's name was Jim, and he gave one ticket to his girlfriend; the other ticket went to Michael. Michael was ecstatic to be spending two weeks in Paris. He and Jim got on well. After the wrap of the film, they decided to go to London to spend time with Michael's affiliate. Michael stopped smoking two weeks before the trip. His appetite grew, and he put on ten pounds.

Michael flew back to Los Angles, noticing the seat in the airplane a bit tighter. Bobby met him at the airport, and they immediately went to an Italian Restaurant in Santa Monica. Michael had clams and linguine. They got home, and it was the end. Michael developed food poisoning from a bad clam, and now, his stomach felt extremely sick. He weathered the storm and was fine the next morning.

The LA office was doing well and continued to make money. Michael started to travel to the desert, Yosemite, the Red Woods, and the coast highway on weekends. He was able to leave LA, and he went every weekend. After a while, it was time for Frances to come to visit. He did not even have to convince her; she was ready. Michael made all the arrangements with the help of Emma. Frances arrived, and she loved the apartment. So, everything was exactly right.

The next few years were smooth for Michael. The LA office was growing rapidly, and Michael took many weekend hiking trips. Somehow, he would find a bench in the wilderness to sit and look at the glorious vista. The New York office was not doing well. Gail had marital problems and was very distracted. The staff used to find her under her desk crying. It was incredibly sad. She built so much of her life on her husband and son, and he walked out for whatever reason.

The horror of AIDS did not end, and friends, business acquaintances, and many more were either diagnosed or dead. Michael's new assistant, Drew, felt strongly about the health crisis. They decided to join the AIDS walk as a company. All the major studios and production companies walked as well. Michael's company raised more money than most of the studios. This tradition of Michael's company participating in the AIDS Walk went on for many years. Michael's involvement with raising money for AIDS was more than just the AIDS Walk. Michael was also an individual donor to the AIDS Quilt.

The quilt project was self-initiated by a family, friend, or companion. They made a quilt and placed on it the name of their departed—sewn or painted in loving words. Michael took a member of his staff to the exhibit who made a quilt for her close friend who had died. This event in Washington D.C. was the largest exhibition of The Quilt, which was spread out on the National Mall. The exhibit had 48,000 panels housing a total of 110,000 names. Michael was also asked to be one of a few activists to host the opening of "And the Band Played On" produced by HBO, presented at the Director's Guild.

Michael produced the 10th Anniversary of Larry Kramer's "Normal Heart" with a member of the original off-Broadway cast at the Coast

Playhouse in West Hollywood. The production was a staged reading of the play, in a theatre that only houses 99 seats. The first week had most of the original cast members reading their roles, though some of the original cast had died. The second week was done with industry names. The reading ran for six performances a week for two weeks. They netted over $25,000 dollars and decided to donate all the funds to the Salk Institute. Salk was making breakthroughs in various medicines that might halt the progression of the disease.

On opening night, Michael got word that a close friend died of AIDS. His parents had kept his illness from his friends, and Michael was devasted. The actions by the parents were common. Many parents thought that the stigma of AIDS would stain their child as well as their family.

That night it rained so hard that the streets were flooded, yet it somehow cleansed the air. Michael started to get angry, and he started to ask, "Why?" Michael asked himself, "Why was there a lack of commitment from the government? Why did parents run away from their children while they were dying? Why did everyone put the truth aside and make the choice to just keep living as if nothing were wrong?"

Michael began looking for an exit, a window, a doorway, something to help him escape this nightmare he found himself in. Outside, the rain was pouring, but he preferred to walk aimlessly in the rain. He did not want to sit in his living room and pretend the disease would go away because it never did. Michael never got depressed. He prided himself on his ability to move on before feeling or thinking of regrets that might stimulate depression.

Michael made friends with some younger male and female clients who demonstrated a more positive view on the human condition. He found the younger men more analytical and able to look deeper into problems. The girls were more optimistic, smart, proactive, and always seemed to have a resolution, which Michael loved. It was so refreshing to hear their hopes for the world.

Michael thought how the young men might subscribe to the 20th century philosopher Husserl's belief, "I doubt, therefore I am." The women might have held on to Descartes in his Cartesian Mediations, "I think, therefore I am." This gave Michael some hope for the future that people, men and women, would want to find the truth, to find their own truths. Once found, the pathway to their freedom is within grasp. They can see the door, there is an exit.

Michael made a crucial decision to adopt a baby. He cared about his mortality. It would give him the ability to pass down his thoughts and beliefs, and more importantly, his love. Michael knew he had to cleanse himself from the soot that gathered on his soul.

Michael was working so hard. He decided he wanted to leave the fruits of his labor to someone he loved, giving him continuous unconditional love. He mentioned the adoption to Bobby, who rudely laughed at him. He continued to get mixed reactions from his friends and family. So, Michael decided to keep this all to himself until he reached his goal.

Michael was going to adopt in South America. He began to make inquiries, but the countries willing to adopt to a single male parent were small. Someone told him about Romania, where a single man did not pose a problem for adoption. Michael found a social worker who would do the reports to the INS and to his chosen country.

His social worker was the best. She was Indian, and her name was Anvi. They met and hit it off as she explained to Michael it would be hard and that if there was another man involved with the adoption, it would be impossible. This was all fine with Michael. The paperwork was immense. They still had not contacted a person in Romania that would help them.

Anvi told Michael they needed to use an American contact who worked with agencies in Romania, as you could not do the process on your own. They met this gentleman, who was very much on the shady side. He had the contacts and told Michael many children have AIDS. Michael did not blink. It rolled off him like water on a duck's back.

The large outbreak of AIDS in the children in Romania was due to unclean needles. Michael just wanted a child. He waited for just a month, and finally, a baby boy was identified. At the same time Michael got a call for an appointment from INS. The government under Bush One was not sympathetic to single male parent adoptions.

He went to the interview with his older sister, who was a cross between Tina Turner and a shrewd woman. She sat in the interview with Michael. The INS women kept asking Michael why he wanted to adopt. The repetitiveness of the questions got a bit ridiculous. His sister interrupted the INS worker while crying and blowing her noise.

She said, "He wants to give and pass on his heritage to a son." She continued to sniffle and occasionally cry.

The INS worker, very frustrated with the conversation with both Michael and his sister, said, "Here are your papers. Go."

Michael walked out of the building, giving his sister a huge hug. She was not crying anymore. Michael was going to be a father.

Michael received a call from Anvi. They identified a child for Michael, and it was a boy. Within a week, Michael received pictures of the baby. It was time to get prepared. Michael booked the flight. It was Christmas, and he thought it would be great to have New Year's Eve in Budapest, Hungary, before proceeding to Romania. Michael felt that all those involved in the adoption would be busy because of the holidays, so he delayed his journey in Budapest. The day after New Year's he would fly to Bucharest, Romania.

New Year's Eve was uneventful. The fireworks were not too spectacular, there were few merry makers on the streets. Michael did get to go to a Hungarian restaurant with violin players and great food. Michael was now prepared to enter Romania, a country who just spontaneously killed their leader of twenty-three years. This execution had only happened four weeks ago after a brief trial found him guilty of crimes against his people.

The plane landed in Bucharest; Michael exited the plane on to the tarmac. As he came down the steps, the field was full of military men with machine guns. Michael thought he needed to leave as soon as possible; he hailed a cab, making sure to que unlike in Lisbon. The ride to the Intercontential Hotel felt like so many adult amusements park rides because of the imperfect roads. He was left off in the street on the driveway of the hotel. He had a long walk to the front door; he got a chance to look around while he walked. The streetlamps were very dim, as were the lights attempting to shine through the windows of the hotel. Off to the left, he saw an ox pulling a cart full of vegetables.

"Oh, God," he said, "this is really an episode of Star Trek. I am in Romania in another dimension."

He made it to lobby but was barely able to make out what he was seeing clearly. At the front desk, he checked in and was given a flashlight. It was better than candles. He was told that the electrical power was reduced by seventy-five percent. Michael got to the room, which was nice. The bed was hard yet adequate.

As he was unpacking, there was a knock on the door. He answered, and it was a young man with a tray of tea and cookies. He came in, smiled, and put the tray down.

Michael asked him, "Why is it so dark inside and outside of the hotel?"

The young man replied in very broken English, "The light is good, but sometimes it goes off. It is nice now." Michael knew these Romanians were good people, even without their lights on.

Michael was to meet the Romanian lawyers that evening at the hotel. He walked around by himself and had lunch in the hotel. He sat at the counter and watched a man be served a turkey leg as big and fat as the man's arm. Michael could not figure out what kind of turkey it was, if in fact it was a turkey.

The lawyer met Michael that evening. She came with her husband. The hotel had a nightclub with wonderful acts to watch, and they invited

Michael to join them. Michael was sure he was on a "Star Trek" set. The first act was a fat man with a whip, and then the bear came out. The bear got on a ball and rolled across the stage.

The second act was a knife thrower with his girl assistant—not even Ed Sullivan could top that act. Michael suggested they go into the lobby for coffee, as he was overwhelmed by the dazzling entertainment. At the table, they attempted to convince Michael not to take the child they assigned him but to take another—a white child. The baby at the hospital was from a gypsy family.

Michael said, "No, this baby is the one I should have."

The lawyer asked if he had the money. Michael said, "Sure."

The lawyer instructed, "When we leave the Hotel, you will walk with us toward my husband's car and throw the money on the seat. I will give the money to the mother when we meet her after court. Tomorrow you will meet your son."

They walked to the car, and Michael dropped the money, which he had in a large envelope as directed by the Romanian lawyer. Large payments for adoption were not legal in

Romania at the time, though the United States recognized the adoption process as legal. If caught by the Romanian police, he and the lawyers would have been in a lot of trouble. The Romanian and her husband could have claimed they did not know Michael, that whatever he was doing he must have the wrong car.

The next morning the lawyer's husband picked Michael up and took him to the hospital where he met his son. Everyone at the hospital was nice to Michael. Before his arrival in Bucharest, Michael sent two exceptionally large boxes of medical supplies—from gauze to aspirin.

The head doctors took Michael to a few wards. One was an AIDS ward; Michael nearly fainted seeing the kids from three to six years old who looked like his friends who also died of AIDS. Their bodies were ravished.

The lawyer took him to another ward of older children, some teenagers, and she told Michael, "These are our Chernobyl children, and they all have leukemia from the fallout. The winds blew into Romania. They are all over Romania, but the government does not want us to talk about these children."

Michael went back to be with his son, and he looked at him and said, "You are safe buddy."

The next day, Michael met the mother. She was a poor street sweeper. She was genuinely nice and humble. She explained why she named her son Nelutu, which meant "Christmas" in Romani, because he was born near the Christmas holiday. Michael told her he would name the baby Joshua after his grandfather, his mother's father. He then went to the embassy to pick up Joshua's green card.

He told the Romanian lawyers he would fly them to the states if they would help him take the baby back to America, since the baby still had to stay for additional checkups before being released. Before he left, he wanted the baby baptized. The lawyer arranged to have Joshua baptized in a Russian Orthodox Church.

The ceremony was long, not to mention the temperature was about 4 degrees. As the priest immersed Joshua, his naked body smoked due to the extreme cold in the church. Michael left Romania and flew to London to stay with his affiliate, who was always so kind to him. Michael rested for two days before going back to LA.

Michael was happy to be going home, but he wanted to help all those children. He left and felt as if he turned his back on them, but he could send something; money and toys for them. Other people would help too, but Joshua needed him more.

CHAPTER SEVENTEEN

1992-1997

Joshua was arriving home. Michael went to the airport with Bobby and Emma. When they arrived at the gate, they were told that the plane would be two hours late. Emma was always good to be around in a minor crisis since she talked a lot and had to find a place to smoke every twenty minutes.

Finally, the doors opened at the gate; the passengers slowly came out. Joshua and the lawyer came out of the plane last. He was home. That was all Michael needed. They got home; Michael had moved to Beverly Hills into a larger house with plenty of rooms for Joshua and guests. Michael planned a big party for friends, clients, and Frances who made a surprise visit.

Michael's staff made all the arrangements for her. She had to be carried on to the plane in her wheelchair, but she was a frequent flyer on MGM Grand, who did so much to make her comfortable. Frances was getting older and sicker. It was truly a surprise she came; Michael was so happy to see her, and he named his son after her father. Frances was happy.

Joshua got so many gifts at the party and through the mail. Michael gathered all the toys and sat Joshua down on the floor. Michael showed each one to Joshua, telling him the individual who gave him each toy. Joshua smiled at each toy.

Michael said to Joshua, "You have so many toys. Let's share them with the hospital in Bucharest."

Joshua appeared to like the idea, but one will never know since he was only three months old. Michael then took all the toys and put them in a huge box, shipping them to the AIDS children in Bucharest. Michael also raised $1,000, which he sent through Western Union to the Bucharest hospital for the Chernobyl Children.

Michael was so happy he was able to do this, and he received so many notes of gratitude from the staff at the hospital. Michael treated Joshua as if he were the second coming. The calmness of his face was so special. In a very spiritual way, Michel knew who Joshua was and what he was feeling and thinking. Michael would lay on a large couch in his living room, put Joshua on his belly, and play Edith Piaf. With a cool breeze coming from his French windows, they both fell asleep loving Piaf.

Michael's nighttime dreams continued; they grew more specific. Michael found out he was a civil engineer in these dreams. He planned housing, but the best thing he designed was a park with statues of huge animals for children. He vacationed in an area that was arid but not a desert. The people in his dream were not people from his real life.

It was hard for him to remember the dreams once he woke up. Even when he was awake, Michal would phase out and enter a semi-sleep state, which put him back into this dream world again. The few people who he shared this with never gave an opinion. They just looked at him and shook their heads in disbelief. Michael never made this phenomenon an issue in his daily life. He kept it to himself. He drew the conclusion it was some alternate reality or a parallel universe. He chose not to think of the dreams too often, but he did visit that same place for the next few years almost every night.

The deaths kept happening. Michael would go to the hospital or the hospice to visit some of his friends. Michael told so many of the victims that it was okay to go. He stayed late to help them even when their companions or family went home for the night. Michael accepted the job of saying goodbye to his friends. After each one of them died, before the nurses and doctors came into the room, Michael just walked down the hall and never looked back.

He would tell them to be calm and say things like, "It is okay. You can go."

What did these victims have to hold onto? No hope, no tomorrow, and no more smiles. Michael had Joshua as his beacon of hope. There were many friends that Michael never said goodbye to, but there were many strangers' hands he held as they were dying in the hospitals. What God would destroy the hopes and ambitions of these young and artistic men? It was not fair, but war is not fair.

A huge snowstorm hit Big Bear, the San Bernardino Mountain Range outside of Los Angles. Michael put Joshua in the car to have him experience snow. Joshua, now one year old, had no idea what was going on, but he smiled, knowing he was secure with his dad. Michael was happy he was outside in the woods.

Suddenly, Michael saw faces in the snow. The faces of people he lost. There were too many spirits standing around in the snow. There was the Ryan Brothers, Gene, and Teddy, who died in Vietnam. He looked for Andy, but he was not there. They all disappeared in the snow as quickly as they came. He looked at Joshua, who was staring at the same area where he saw the images of friends. Did he see them too? The occurrence was another indication that Michael was obsessed with those he lost.

During the next few weeks, Michael decided to adopt another child, a girl. He called the Romanian lawyers and Anvi. Anvi did paperwork with the government, and they believed they had a girl available for adoption. Michael made plans. Bobby volunteered to join him on this trip, Michael could use help.

They left for Romania. They were met at the airport and told they must go to court as soon as possible. They got to the court directly from the airport. Outside the court, there were a handful of Romanians carrying their babies approaching any foreigner asking them to buy their child. They were extremely aggressive and unaware of the adoption procedures in Romania.

Michael said to the lawyers, "You are not bringing me here to find a child."

They pushed him into the court. His name was finally called, and he went up to the judge, who approved his paperwork for a potential adoption. The lawyer told him they located a child who was just born. They rushed to the hospital, and the baby was angelic. The baby's mother was about seventeen years old. He went to her house. She lived with her grandmother. She understood everything. They were to meet the next day to exchange money.

The next afternoon, all three of them were standing on the street—the lawyer, the mother, and Michael, who gave her the money. The mother was anxious to leave. The lawyer told Michael to kiss the mother. Michael kissed her on the cheek, assuming it was a gesture of goodwill, but instead she slapped him.

Michael was shocked, and he looked at the lawyer in anger. "Why did you say to do that?"

Michael should have said 'no,' but he did it. It was the wrong advice. The mother was angry.

The next day the baby was stolen from the hospital. They finally found the baby with her mother at another hospital. Michael did not like the situation. He told them it would be better to find another child and let her raise her baby.

"No," they all told Michael.

The baby got extremely sick, and no one at the hospital told Michael what the problem was. Michael asked if the priest who baptized Joshua could come to the hospital and baptize the baby. The priest came, and they had a small orthodox ceremony. The reason the baby got sick was because the baby drank bad milk from the mother.

The next morning, the baby was missing again. Michael had to be in London on business, so they told him to go. When they found the baby, they would bring her to the states. Michael went to the U.S. Embassy and got her a green card with surprisingly no problems. They assured Michael not to worry because she would be found.

Michael was back in London; he received a call that the baby was found. The mother took her to the Port city of Castanza, Romania. The mother sold her to a group of Romani people. They were able to get the baby back. The lawyer would call Michael when they were back in Bucharest.

254

The lawyers and the baby arrived in Los Angles with fanfare that equaled Joshua's. They named the beautiful little girl Elizabeth Louise. The name Elizabeth had no special meaning. Michael loved the name. The name Louise was testament to numerous family members of Michael's, who either were named Louis or Louise. The two babies got along as well as his three dogs.

Elizabeth was given an equal, if not greater, welcome than Joshua. The party was great. Michael kept telling guests that they did not have to bring gifts, but the gifts and toys poured in. Michael did the same thing as he did with Joshua. He collected some of the gifts and put them in a huge box, sending it off to Bucharest hospital.

Michael had a real family—two children, three dogs, a bird, and two cats that lived under the house. Michael's housekeeper took care of the children. She did not speak English. She had worked for Michael for five years as a housekeeper before she became the Nanny. Michael spoke broken Spanish, but he believed she secretly spoke English all that time. He was fond of her; she was a good worker who loved the children and the animals.

One morning, Bobby came downstairs and told Michael he quit his job; Michael was shocked. Michael asked, "You are making four figures weekly, and you left the job?"

Bobby said he was going to watch the kids and work for a florist. Michael harshly asked, "What do you know about flowers? I do all the gardening here. You never did anything."

"I watched you," said Bobby.

"Look, your income will be lost. How are we to make up the loss?" Michael asked.

Bobby said, "Look, I would be better at watching the kids and taking them around."

Michael was losing his patience. "But who hired you for this job?"

Bobby said, "I really love these kids. Who better to be with them?"

Michael said, "I love the kids more, but I did not leave my company. Why don't I get to make that choice? Why would you get to make that choice?"

The next morning Michael gave Bobby an apron and said, "Welcome to the domestic staff. I took down the ad for a Beverly Hills Housewife. Don't forget the flowers." Michael was terribly angry Bobby was going to continue to live off him but now to a greater degree.

Michael decided to get out of town for a small vacation. A friend offered him a house in Italy for no charge. The house was in a small town in Tuscany, Monte in Chanti.

Michael said, "Sure."

He had realized that this could be a very cheap trip, he had free upgrades for plane tickets, and he had a credit with the rental car company. Michael gathered the kids and off they went without the animals, but somehow, Bobby invited himself. They got to the house, which was a bumpy and long ride off the main road. They found themselves in a field of grape vines.

They finally got to the house. It was a shepherd's house—very primitive but great. Michael had a large separate bedroom downstairs that was designed like the Arabian Nights. He spent many days with the children playing stories about Prince Turhan, Ali Baba, Aladdin, and the Sultan and Dinarzad. Michael had as much fun as the children.

Two days into the stay, there was a knock at the door. It was Bobby's cousin and her husband. They stayed for a week; it was extremely uncomfortable for Michael. They left, and Michael was able to continue having magical adventures in the Arabian room with his kids.

They had a great vacation and stayed for a month. Then, it was back to work. They got into a routine in the house. That was brilliant. Michael went to the office, Elsa the housekeeper looked after the children's needs, and Bobby went with all the mothers to the various groups like the gym, swimming lessons, and singing group. This went on for a long time.

Michael's business was not doing that well, and neither was the New York office. Michael made a few bad loans to clients. He needed to bail out the New York office, so he sold his land in Ojai and took a majority portion of his father's inheritance and put it into the company.

The infusion helped, but it did not solve the problem. He then learned that his company accountant, Jerry, had a warrant for embezzlement. He traced Jerry's actions in the company, and since he did not directly handle money, the company was safe.

Michael moved to a new house in the LA area, cutting his overhead by twenty five percent and it was great for everyone. His children were doing well. Bobby asked Michael if he could borrow $5,000 dollars. Michael asked him why, he said his American Express bill got out of hand, and he wanted to fly his mother up from Alabama with her sister. He was hoping Michael could pay for their trip as Michael did on numerous occasions.

Michael said, "No, things are not going that well. Our bookings in the company are down, and New York is in the pits."

Gail had to miss two paychecks; she was hysterical, screaming and crying. A few weeks passed. Bobby told Michael he made the reservations for his mother and aunt to arrive in one week. Michael did not know how Bobby paid for the trip. He became concerned. He went through his accounts and remembered he put one account with Bobby as co-signature in case something happened to him. Bobby cleaned out the account. He calmly approached Bobby and asked him if he took money from the account.

Bobby said, "Yes, my name was on it. Why couldn't I?"

"Because it was for an emergency, not for you to spend as you like," Michael said, truly angry. You didn't even ask me. How dare you." Michael said, "Bobby, I want you to leave. I cannot trust you. You took a liberty that was not yours. Tell your mother she cannot come unless you have a friend she can stay with. Take the credit from the airline tickets and apply it to the company for future airline tickets. Your actions made this house even more financially insecure. Do not ever come into this house again. I never want to see you."

Bobby became another person after this incident. He told anyone who would listen how hurt he was not being with the children. Michael was receiving calls from friends and clients expressing their concern for Bobby. Bobby knew exactly what he was doing. Michael did not change his position.

A few of Michael's staff members came over to his house. Suddenly, the phone rang. It was Bobby telling everyone he was going to die. They asked him where he was. To Michael's shock, he was on the property at Ojai. Michael failed to tell him he sold the property, the staff that were at the house pleaded to Bobby, over the phone, to come home. Bobby was very stubborn.

The phone rang, and it was a client asking if they watched the local news on ABC. He said a helicopter was flying over one of the mountains in Ojai. Bobby was going to jump. Michael was concerned for Bobby's safety. The staff checked if the business name was mentioned but it was not. Everyone said it was only Bobby's name that they said on the news. Someone in the background on the phone said they mentioned Michael's name.

Michael and a few of his staff members drove up to Ojai, asking a friend of Bobby's, Stephen, to meet them at the property to take Bobby to his home. At the gate of the property was the real estate agent and new owner, who lacked compassion.

He said, "If you don't end this now, I will sue you and this guy on the cliff for trespassing."

They quickly got Bobby down. This just added insanity to Michael's life. What he would give to be back talking to Reservoir Men. With Bobby out of the house, Michael had to adjust. The children would ask where Bobby was. Michael comforted them.

In a few days, the children were able to move on as well. Michael hired a real Nanny with a car. Maria, the new Nanny, worked well with the children, and they loved her. She also had a good relationship with Elsa and Michael.

Michael put his time and energy into fixing the company. He streamlined the assistants and expense accounts. He attempted to talk to Gail about the actual financial condition of the company, but the conversation lasted for less than ten minutes. Michael was low on savings. He asked Bobby to pay him back for the money he took, but somehow, Bobby thought that the money was his.

Michael estimated that sixty percent of the startup money was paid back to him through expenses, though his constant underwriting was never addressed. Michael forgot about it in time. Gail met a new boyfriend, and it looked profoundly serious. He owned a large fashion company and was attempting to raise additional capital to expand his company. The agency's problems were not in line with her future husband's agenda. If she could issue payroll to the New York staff, she was content. Michael had to shoulder all the problems of the company by himself.

Susan was Michael's new bookkeeper; she also handled all financial aspects for the company. She worked for two large film studios, but she wanted to work with Michael. He always worked hard to help her check that the books were both accurate and honest. She took a salary below what she was earning at her other jobs.

Susan was very disturbed with Gail's noninvolvement with the company's finances. She did confront her one day, explaining to Gail how it was important for her as an owner to know what was happening on the financial side within the company. They arranged to talk every Wednesday. Gail made the first appointment but cancelled all the other appointments. The staff believed Gail knew exactly what was happening in the company, including the dwindling income and the amount of money being drawn by the New York office; she was just playing dumb.

Michael lost two casting director friends while he was attempting to restructure his company, but he found the time to go to the hospital for one of them. The other had no money left. He was a powerful casting director. His former partner would send him meatloaf sandwiches, which he loved before he got sick. Now, he could not eat them. He weighed about ninety pounds and developed a Swedish rash. The rash consisted of exceedingly small dots covering his body in mass. This condition had not been seen in America for an exceptionally long time. Michael would regularly see him at the hospice until he died peacefully with a tear coming down his cheek.

Michael befriended a guy about his age. He was a nice Mormon guy. Bill was an actor, a good one at that. Michael told him he needed to get his feet wet by taking a proactive role within the community and by doing some project or charity. Michael always wanted to do a reading series of scripts like they did with plays in New York.

Michael got the space, and they solicited scripts. The series became remarkably successful as soon as they started. They attracted semi-names in the business to do the readings, and they were sold out at all their performances. Michael was enormously proud of Bill's success, but there was a cloud of doom and gloom over him. This bothered Michael, as he could not figure out what his problem was.

The children were doing very well. Joshua both did academically well in school and was great at playing baseball. Elizabeth seemed like she did everything from soccer to softball, but she really excelled in art. Her early drawings were spectacular. She had a mind of her own, was very opinionated, and was extremely politically progressive at her early age. They began in private school for kindergarten, but Michael was uncomfortable since most of the schoolmates were from privileged households. Michael did not want them to grow up with any attitude that sprung from being privileged, he moved them to a great public school.

Michael was going into his office, and a waiter from the restaurant across the street came running over, telling him to keep away from his Mormon friend, Bill. Michael could not understand why he was so concerned.

He turned to Michael and told him, "He does or did porno."

Michael dismissed this, saying, "A few actors' venture into this when they first come to LA, but it is noticeably short lived. I am sure this is the case with Bill."

This statement stayed with Michael for weeks. He did not want to seek advice from anyone, but he was sure the explanation he gave the waiter was correct. Bill came from such a nice family, and he was just a nice guy that was highly intelligent. Michael could not let it go.   One day, Michael got into his car and ventured into West Hollywood, stopping at several porn shops. He went in and started to look at the VHS tapes on the shelf. He then noticed Bill's picture on several tape jackets. He visited at least two other shops and discovered increasingly more tapes with Bill. He estimated that he made a lot of porno films. He talked to an agent in his office who was into porn and was told Bill was quite a star among those who looked at porn. Michael said to himself, "How would I know?"

He was not concerned with his own image, but what would people think of him with two children? He did not want to hurt Bill, nor did he expect Bill to tell him on first meeting, "Oh, by the way...I did porn."

Michael went to Bill and told him what he found out but asked Bill not to give him an explanation. Michael told him it was not a good idea that Bill and Michael were friends because of his dealings in pornography. Michael told Bill that he would be happy to continue the script readings, as Bill was now producing them, and any acting role the office could secure for him. That was the end of Bill. He left suddenly without a goodbye.

266

CHAPTER EIGHTEEN

1997-1998

Bill was gone; the house was quiet. Michael had his life to himself. All his choices were his alone. He loved being with his children. The love of his children was the greatest. Simply getting them a small gift and watching their eyes and happiness for a tiny "something" filled him with joy. He always went to the movies with them, without being discreet with the ratings of the films.

The best was going out to dinner with the children. They had many favorite restaurants. They loved Chinese, Mexican, and simple American cuisine. After dinner, it was frozen yogurt. Sweets were never a large staple in their diets, but grapes and all types of berries were. Many nights, they would sleep with Michael, especially Joshua. He was afraid Michael would not be there in the morning, so it was easier to keep watch in

Michael's bed. Joshua also suffered from night terrors.

Elsa, the housekeeper, went in Joshua's room one night while Michael was out, and she saw a woman sitting on the side of Joshua's bed. Elsa was religious. She was not afraid, but believed the woman was attempting to tell Joshua something. These shadows would happen more than a few times. So, between these apparitions and Michael's other dimension dream-world, Michael had a lot to think about.

The world around Michael seemed a little disjointed. His staff seemed not exactly right, but the New York office was doing better. However, there was a distance towards Michael and the staff. One night, Michael had to return to the office and found all the assistants and his new bookkeeper looking at files. It was late. He asked them what they were doing, as business was slow, and they should be home. He became paranoid. His personal assistant was also there but looking guilty, as if he did not want to be there. Michael saw the boxes with all the financial data from the company sitting in the corner of his office. He told Robert, his assistant, to take the four boxes to his home and put them in his garage.

Michael left the office, telling his staff never to do this again since the office was not their playground. Four days later, he passed the office and saw the lights on. He went into the office only to see the staff there again—minus his assistant. He told them if this happens again, they would all be fired. He had the utmost trust for his assistant and noticed that when Robert brought the boxes to his house they were never tampered with—the seals were intact. This incident with the staff aimlessly doing nothing in the office was genuinely concerning to Michael, and it only reinforced his feelings of uneasiness.

Feeling the disconnect, Michael got the children from school, told them they were going on a trip, and that they were leaving right away. They got home, and Michael told Elsa that she could go home. They were ready to leave. Elsa reminded them about the dogs. She asked who was going to watch and feed them. She told Michael she would stay at the house until they got back.

As they were driving off, Joshua said, "You did not tell us where we are going."

Michael stared at Joshua. "Oh my, how could I not have told you? Yosemite, guys! And we are staying at the Ahwahnee Hotel. I want to hike a lot. We can go to the Half Dome and Glacier Point and see the falls."

Yosemite was the best place in the world especially for Michael since he had an annual pass to Yosemite and two nights free at the hotel. Michael's favorite thing to do was to get up about 6 am, walk outside of the hotel, sit on a log shaped bench, and watch the morning mist cover the ground. He would sit there for about 2 hours.

The experience was peaceful. He felt more at one with himself. There was not a past or a future while he sat on the bench. This was his bubble of solitude. Michael would have loved to take this feeling back home with him. After this, Michael would get the children and go downstairs to the great dining hall made completely of lumber to have a fabulous breakfast.

On one memorable hike with the children, Michael was walking through the forest and became very aware of the stillness around him. He turned and saw Joshua standing right next to a wolf. The wolf was looking at Joshua, and Joshua was looking at the wolf. It stayed that way for a while. Michael quietly told Joshua to move, as he took a photo.

"Let's get back to the hotel for dinner."

The ride home was only about the wolf and the snowman that Elizabeth built. With the many trips they had taken with Michael, this was the best for all three of them. They got home but insisted they go to the local drugstore to develop the photos they took. They wanted to take them to school the next day.

The photo of Joshua and the wolf became legendary at school and Elizabeth's snowman as well, with his red scarf. The photos of the wolf and the snowman were placed on the bulletin board in their classrooms. Michael now had to get back to some form of reality, dealing with a bleaker and more dismal world.

Michael's alternate reality dreams got more real and specific. He spoke to several doctors, who explained to him that he created this realm in his subconscious to get away from his world. The alternate reality was like a vacation from his current state of being. It made sense since this all started when Andy died, and it got more severe when all his friends got sick. The truth was that Michael was much happier here, even in this difficult reality, than his alternate dream space. He decided to stay.

Now the problems he was encountering here, were with the office. Even though he had an answer as to their origins, the dreams did not end. His drinking got worse. He never got drunk, only significantly high, he was proud he could drink as much as seven vodka martinis and not feel it. He started to smoke again. Joshua and Elizabeth got very mad at him for smoking. Michael always prided himself for never getting depressed, but he was close to it. Since there was no one to talk to, so much was internalized. The truth was that Michael was never flush with money his entire life, outside of receiving his father's inheritance, he always struggled. The bad part was that most of his father's inheritance went to underwriting the office.

Susan, the former bookkeeper for the office called Michael and asked him out for lunch. Susan had been gone from the office for several months. Her health was getting bad, as she was diagnosed with MS. She told Michael at lunch that Gail was very aware of the financial condition of the office, and it was her inability to get involved that was hurting the progress of the office toward healing. "She had to pay her share." Business was bad, and that was what partners do.

Michael felt despondent, and he told Susan he cashed the children's savings bonds he purchased, which totaled about $20,000. He put half in the New York office and half in the Los Angeles office. Susan said she understood what he did, but this was not even enough to hold the dike in place.

After lunch, Susan kissed Michael on the cheek and said, "Continue loving your wonderful children, but I believe you must handle this the right way with Gail." Michael immediately went back to the office and prepared a financial report for Gail that was simplistic and hopefully easy for Gail to understand.

The next day, Michael got Gail on the phone, and she took a half an hour to tell Michael about two of the opening night parties she went to that week. Michael told her that they were at a point in the business where they either had to sell it or just wind down the company slowly. Gail did not say anything. She just listened to him. He told her the money he put into the company was never fully paid back and that he was carrying the ball for all these years. At that point in the conversation, she got annoyed and told Michael that he was the one who wanted to open in LA. She felt that was his problem.

"But what about the money I put into New York?" asked Michael.

"I have no money." said Gail, curtly.

Michael said he could produce a plan to make the company whole while seeking outside funds. Gail's response blew Michael away.

"I do not think anyone I know would invest in this company."

Michael thought, "Do you believe in our company, or is it all the opening nights and parties you believe in?" Michael talked for about an hour, and Gail had no compassion toward the issues. When they finished the phone call, Michael finally realized Gail would have preferred to just to run the New York office and to hell with LA. But it was LA that garnished the respect of the industry. It developed and maintained several large industry names. In the last eight years, Gail had only come out to LA three or four times, she complained that the agents in LA did not like her, so she felt unwelcome.

Michael said to her, "How can you feel unwelcome in your own company?" Michael now knew what he was working with, and it was not a partner. Michael did not know what to do now that

Gail was acting this way. Should he resign? Should Gail leave? Could they break up the two offices? He kept going over and over it again in his mind, he remembered Dostoevsky's famous quote, "A man of intellect does not act." He had to make a move.

It was not just the condition of the office that unsettled Michael; it was a general lack of commitment by people. Any conversation with Gail became nonexistent. Michael was friendly with one of the agents in the New York office, but his distance toward Michael grew. The agents in the LA office spoke to Michael about an impending audit concerning the misappropriation of funds. Michael knew nothing of this. He had a good network into the entertainment community.

This uneasiness lasted for several months. Michael would hear rumors of trouble within his business, which was alien to him since he knew about the situation with Gail but nothing else. The holidays were approaching. Michael usually had a big Christmas party for his clients, but he felt it would be better to go to New York.

Frances was getting sicker, and the children wanted to see the family. Michael and the children went Christmas shopping in Los Angeles and got everyone in the family something, even the cousins in New York. The family decided to have a limit on the gifts—except for Frances. The children attempted to wrap some of the gifts. They were strange wrappings since Michael was also bad at wrapping, so they ran out and bought Christmas bags. They decided to leave on Christmas day and celebrate Christmas Eve at the house because the west coast Santa would not know where to deliver Joshua and Elizabeth's gifts.

The children had a great Christmas Eve. Santa came early somehow. He got into the house while they were at dinner. What a surprise when they came home! After they opened all their gifts, they went right to bed for only three hours. They woke up, and they were on a red eye to New York that night. They got to the airport and Michael told the kids that when they take off, if they look out the widow, they will see Santa leaving for Hawaii in the night sky. Joshua swore he saw him, but Elizabeth did not buy into it.

Landing in New York was exciting. The driver was waiting at the luggage carousel. They went to the hotel in downtown Brooklyn, a nice hotel right across from the state and federal courthouses. Getting into the hotel was great especially since it was heavily discounted. Their room was large, and they all had separate beds.

Michael packed all the gifts, rented a car, and went off to his sister's house, where the whole family would gather for dinner. Frances could not go; her legs were bad. Michael told the children they would have a special day with grandma the next day. Frances was incredibly happy to see them the next day.

They had a wonderful time at Michael's sister's home. Both of his sisters and two nieces heard from Bobby, who told them how horrible Michael was to him.

Michael said, "Nice Christmas greeting, sis."

Bobby claimed that Michael would not give him anything—including some of his personal belongings. Bobby also complained that he had not seen the children for at least a year. Michael explained to his family that Bobby stole money from him and stopped working, that Michael was picking up his bills. It was not fair to help someone who just wanted to be a Beverly Hills house mate and live off him.

Michael felt like his family did not believe him, how could they take a stranger's side over his? The exact same situation happened with his London affiliate. Bobby called her and told her the same story, and she decided to stop working with

Michael for no apparent reason. All Michael could say was that it was bullshit.

The day with Frances was great, but she did not look well. Frances was dazed. She told Michael a story of how Mexicans were singing to her from the TV screen, and one was Andy, who was not Mexican. Michael was empathetic, telling Frances to tell Andy how much he missed him. Frances told Michael that his sister was not nice to her when she needed help. Michael hoped this was not true but was glad they got her a full-time companion. They gave Frances kisses galore and went back to the hotel.

The next day was solely for the children. They saw the tree at Rockefeller Center, they went ice skating, ate at Jecklye and Hyde, and never wanted to leave. The next day, Michael called the New York office only to find out Gail decided to close the office till New Years. This was not typical; Michael always kept a skeleton staff for those workdays between Christmas and New Year's.

Michael had lunch the next day with a friend that worked at the union. He told Michael to watch out, that something was happening in reference to his business. Michael pleaded with him to tell him anything he might know; it must be a rumor. The next day, they flew back to LA, feeling like he was going back to a possible sinking ship.

Michael had a lovely New Year's Eve. He cooked a light supper, had plenty of drinks, and went back to smoking. The martinis and smoking were the best. Only twelve close friends were with Michael that night. They all made Michael feel secure and accepted. His party guests left at about 1 am. The children were in bed. Michael sat in one of the gardens on a bench, reflecting on what life had brought his way.

Susan suddenly came back in, forgetting her package. Michael invited her to sit in the garden with him for a moment. "What a journey," Michael said, "You want to know my truth? I am a man. I am a man who wants to love and be loved, who cares, and who is willing to help people. I believe in kindness. I must protect my own space. I am a man who knows when to say 'no.' And there are those who invade my integrity. I survived trial by fire, trial by water, and all the trials that people have thrown at me so far. I stand alone, proud of all my actions. Susan, I am free, free of the Reservoir Men, free of people who want but do not give. I am free of all the magic, mystery, and mysticism of religion. I truly have communion with the Thou. I am a man and proud of it, no matter what comes."

Without a word, tears in her eyes, Susan stood up from the bench, hugged Michael, and quietly left. Michael looked up at the stars and imagined the amount of people in and out of his life. The number of them was so immense, like the stars in the sky. What a great party that would have been if they all came down here, laughed, and loved with him.

Michael slowly walked upstairs to his bedroom. He passed Elizabeth's room, kissed her on the head, and wished her a happy New Year. Then, he passed Joshua's room.

He walked to Joshua's bed and took his hand, shook it, and said, "That is what guys do, shake hands." But Michael was emotional and kissed him on the forehead too. Michael slowly walked to his bedroom, undressed, fell on his bed, and slept.

On New Year's Day, the children went with Michael to brunch in Venice and walked on the boardwalk. For dinner, they ate at their favorite Chinese restaurant in West Hollywood. Arriving home, they noticed someone sitting on the porch. Michael quickly got out of the car and went over to the man. It was Joe, a young client of Michael's.

Two years earlier, Michael brought Joe into the agency as a client; they had a very respectful relationship. Joe asked Michael if he had time to talk. Normally, Michael would have asked Joe if it could wait till the next day, but Michael saw the urgency in his tone. He told Joe to come in and to give him some time to put the children to bed.

Michael came back into the living room with a martini for himself and his guest. He finally broke down and had liquor in his house. Joe sat down and told Michael to listen before he commented. He told Michael that there was an action to take over the office, and his LA staff were aware of it, as well as the New York staff. Gail had also secured a replacement for Michael to run the LA office. The clients were not informed. She was waiting for the proper time after Michael left the office. Gail had secured all the bank statements and hired a lawyer.

Michael was shocked. "Who told you, Joe? Do you know a timetable for when she intends to do this?"

Joe said he was dating someone at the union who told him, and he was not aware of a time she was going to act on this. Joe seemed very pale; Michael became concerned about Joe's health, asking him how his T-cell count was. Joe did not respond to much of anything.

"There is nothing you can do," said Michael.

"Just be healthy. There are some experimental drugs. Stay away from AZT. That is AIDS by prescription."

Joe finished his drink and got up to leave. Joe hugged Michael, and while he was holding on to Michael, he whispered in his ear, "I'm scared. What is going to happen?"

Michael replied, "You are going to live and have fun. Just be gay." They both laughed. Before Joe left, he stopped in the doorway, turning to Michael.

"What's wrong Joe?" asked Michael.

"I did not call. I wanted to."

"Why didn't you?" said Michael, staring at the young man, who was in a world of anxiety and apprehension.

"I was afraid they tapped your phone," said Joe, and he left.

CHAPTER NINETEEN

1998-1999

The first thing Michael did when he got into the office was hire a lawyer. His company's corporate lawyer referred him to two lawyers. They were two exceptionally good lawyers. Michael had an intense meeting. One of the lawyer's sons owned a talent agency, so he knew the ins and outs of the operations of an agency.

In the passing weeks, his LA staff became very distant. In a matter of a few days, the lawyers got back to Michael and confirmed everything Joe told him and much more. Gail wanted Michael out of the office in three weeks. He was not to spend any more time in the office without the consent of her lawyer. Gail decided not to demand an audit of the books, realizing it would make her look bad. The company's accountant was to report to Gail only.

Michael told his lawyers, "Gail was crazy. What did she know about the company? She had blinders on for ten years, drawing substantial and consistent pay checks from the company even as Michael put his own personal money in to keep it afloat."

Gail's plan was devised by her new husband 'to be' with his Wall Street yuppie mentality. In the weeks following, Gail refused to countersign any LA checks to clients, which created another problem. The rumors were flying. A friend of Michael's lied to the trade newspapers that the missing money was more than a million dollars. He was not a friend anymore.

Every day the cracks grew. The situation became a stalemate, and the agency was nonoperative. Three weeks passed, and Michael did not resign. Suddenly, a fax came from the union, requesting an audit to discover any irregularities. This was a blessing in disguise, thought Michael. Some of this craziness would be on hold for a while, and the clients could be serviced.

Michael was hoping this audit would discover the truth. Unfortunately, three very destructive assistants blew the situation out of proportion with misinformation. These assistants claimed that they heard a rumor that the police

284

were involved with this situation, which was false. Within two hours, these lying staff members decided to physically destroy the office Michael had worked so hard to build for ten years. They threw files out of the file cabinets, they broke a computer, they shredded papers. Michael was at home when his assistant called to tell him what happened.

He said to himself, "This is all over. The end!"

Michael asked the nanny to stay the night, as he was not well. He went to bed in the late afternoon and got up the next morning with someone tapping on his shoulder.

It was Susan saying, "Get out of that bed and take a shower. We are going to the office to meet with these auditors that the unions hired. Remember, Michael, you did nothing wrong though it feels that you did. For three years, I took care of the books, and I know what really happened here. Gail was in New York with her terrible attitude, and she killed the company. Let's go to the office. I'll drive."

Michael got to the office and was shocked to finally see the level of destruction. The whole office was destroyed—files, papers, and desks all thrown everywhere. The building's office manager came into the office to talk to Michael.

He looked at Susan and asked her "What animals did this? Who was right or wrong is not the issue. The issue is respect. Who is going to clean this up?"

Susan said proudly, "Michael and I will take care of it within the week." The union auditors waked in and just looked around in amazement. They asked Michael if he made this mess.

Michael said, "No, I guess it was the staff."

The auditors look surprised, and they shook their heads in amazement. Michael walked into the office with Susan and the auditors. They closed the door. Michael spent at least six hours with the auditors. He told Susan to go home, as he noticed her physical condition was taxed. Michael walked her to the door, and she gave him a kiss on the cheek. She reminded him that he did nothing wrong.

The auditors left with all the check books and the general ledger. They were given the contacts at the bank. They were mostly surprised that Gail was operating the New York office with only one checking account and not a separate account for the actor's trust. The actor's trust account was a banking account where an agency received all the monies to be paid to the actor, which was then paid to the performer from the trust. They asked Michael who controlled the New York account.

Michael said, "Gail does. She prepares all the deposits and tells the bookkeeper, Susan, what bills are to be paid. Other than that, her interactions were extremely limited with Susan."

Michael told the auditors that the new bookkeeper was hired to replace Susan due to her health. Jane, the new bookkeeper, worked on her own. She did not care for Michael because he was always pushing her to get work done.

Michael's lawyers attempted to talk with Gail's lawyers, but they were arrogant. Gail attempted to have a relationship with the union auditors for the sole purpose of knowing when they planned to arrest Michael. Michael spent at least two days a week at the office of the auditors, explaining why certain actions were done. They developed a trusting relationship over the course of time.

Gail was getting married, and she told the union lawyers and the auditors not to bother her while preparing her wedding or while on her wonderful month-long honeymoon in Europe! This was the first time they cast an opinion about Gail, saying, "Doesn't she care?" Gail was simply devising plans to fully control the situation from her honeymoon suite. They had to wonder why she never got on a plane to her office in LA.

The audit was complete, and the short fall was $168,000 and $150,000 in receivables. The auditors felt that if Michael could collect the $150,000 in receivables due to the company, he could zero out the balance sheet. They would present this to the state and the union as a proposal. The meeting was scheduled in two weeks. During all this chaos, Michael was informed that his assistant, Drew, of five years and a friend of many more years died of AIDS in Mexico while teaching ESL. His former assistant fought off his AIDS affliction for so many years and survived. This loss was devastating to Michael during an already challenging time.

About a week before the meeting, Michael was in his garage. He remembered those four boxes of cancelled checks that his assistant took from the office. Michael painfully remembered his three assistants and bookkeeper were attempting to gather information against Michael going through corporate books and private emails.

Michael decided to call the auditors and ask them if they wanted the boxes. They suggested to bring them in. Michael opened the first box, and to his astonishment, he found ten checks sitting on the top of the box. They were his checks written on Michaels checking account made out to the company for a total of $210,000. The next morning, he brought them in to the auditors. They were shocked. The auditors were successfully able to verify the checks, making sure that they were deposited in one of the LA or New York business accounts.

The day of the meeting, Michael was with his two lawyers. At the other end of the table was his new bookkeeper, Jane. Neil, the auditor, got up and gave an accounting of the balance sheet and all the receivables. He also added that he questioned Gail's intent.

Neil stated, "Gail acts as if she does not care what the outcome is." Saying more to himself, "As long as Michael goes to jail, that is her sole objective."

Neil then produced the $210,000 in cancelled checks; money given to the company by

Michael. There was a buzz in the room. Jane got up and grabbed the checks from a member of the committee and did not want to give them back. Michael's lawyer's faces were empty. Now Michael realized that even they were hoping he was guilty so they could fight a trial in the media.

They looked at Michael, excused themselves from the room, and went into the waiting room. No one said anything to Michael, but he knew he was no longer the bad guy that everyone could tear down. They all had to reset their perceptions, which proved difficult for them to do because people liked to blame the bad guy, even when he was vindicated.

After a few minutes, Michael realized that his lawyers were never returning to the room. In fact, they left disappointed. They wanted the press and the coverage. Now they were out looking for the next bad guy to raise their profile. The union committee agreed with Neil that the union should form a custodial agreement with Michael, collecting the receivables and leaving the money in the custodial account until most of the receivables were collected. Michael left the meeting, alone. The union and Neil asked Gail to join the custodial agreement, but of course, she refused; she was leaving for a month in Europe.

Michael and Neil were highly successful in collecting the receivables. Michael told Neil there was one client that owed just under $10,000 dollars to the company. Neil called up their manager, who claimed they paid it about a month ago to Gail. Neil asked for the cancelled check. He received it via fax immediately and saw the endorsement was to Gail for an account in Scarsdale, New York that was formed under the company's original EIN number without Michael's knowledge.

Neil called the bank and found out Gail opened the account with the EIN number of Michael and Gail's company and was diverting receivables to the new secret account. The union was not happy at all. They sued Gail. Gail found the lawsuit the day she came back from Europe on her doorstep. The union lawyers called Gail's lawyer. He told them that Gail was just going on the advice of her new husband. These actions concerning the secret bank account turned the tide of the situation.

There was a general feeling with the people involved that suspicions were changing from Michael to Gail. One of Michael's LA agents, who was friendly with the bookkeeper, and obviously Gail, hooked up with three corporate vendors who were owed money and petitioned the court to declare involuntary bankruptcy on the company. This would have prevented any further collection of receivables and get Gail off the hook for a while. Michael handled this situation in court by himself.

Michael appealed to the court, "If this was granted, it would hurt so many people who would never receive their money." The judged dismissed the request for involuntary bankruptcy.

The IRS now started to question Gail. They did not ask her about the non-filed last quarter withholding taxes, but how she set up this venture in Scarsdale, New York. Gail was terribly upset, claiming she had no idea how this happened!

The auditors did not believe Gail's accusations because Michael personally gave the company close to $350,000 out of his own pocket—of which only $190,000 dollars was paid back. He got most of the money from the sale of the Ojai property and his father and mother's trust, which was wiped out. He never received the missing six months' salary during the writer's strike. Michael only applied expense reimbursements to pay himself back what was rightfully owed to him.

The one-time Michael asked Gail for some type of company pay back to him on time structured payments, she said to him, "We have no money."

Michael discovered later that Gail was paying her daughter's private school tuition and large vendors she personally owed out of the New York checking account right before the breakup of the company.

When Michael confronted her, Gail said, "This is what is owed to me."

Michael responded, "No. You are taking my family's money, which I was using to make my company whole again."

She was a partner that could not tell you about the balance in the checking account. Within a matter of two days, her new husband came downstairs to her beautiful office in their luxurious house and told her to pack her belongings, take her child, and be out in twenty-four hours. The IRS made it too hot for Gail's husband. With his new companies, he did not want the negative publicity with either the public or the IRS. Gail called her mother and made plans to go to Arizona to be with her. She left in the cab that next morning. Her husband told her she would hear from his lawyers about an annulment. Some of Michael's friends urged him to take out an ad in the entertainment papers telling his story.

"No, what will that do? The best thing to do is to let this conversation go away in the public eye until it is not hot news anymore," said Michael. "The argument is better served amongst the professionals looking into the situation, not the public."

Michael did get a chance to see Richard, his former friend whom he inadvertently hurt when he revealed Richard had AIDS. They accidently met in a Chinese restaurant with his children. Michael apologized for his indiscretion. Richard told Michael to be quiet.

He looked down at Michael's children and said, "You did a wonderful thing." He died of AIDS four months later.

Michael sold the house. The new rental house Michael got was great for him and the children, lots of room but limited backyard—but enough for a trampoline. Charity, one of Michael's dogs, had to be put to sleep at sixteen years old. His other dog Pepper ran away because he thought he was next. Michael brought in a stray dog, Maria, who started to eat all the wood in the house, even though she was not teething. They found a home for Maria.

One day Michael and the children came home to find a golden retriever in their backyard. The kids named her Jessie. Somehow, after four months living with them, Jessie was robbed in the backyard while they were having dinner in the house. At night, the children believed they heard Jessie barking up the block. Michael would have loved to agree with them, but he did not want to open a complex issue like who stole Jessie with the children.

One night, extremely late, Michael walked up the block to find Jessie in the house of a neighbor where they all believed the barking came from. Michael knocked on the door, and three little children opened the door with Jessie barking in the background. Michael smiled and told the children what a great dog they had. He knew that Jesse must have run away, and the children must have found her. Bringing Jessie back to New York would have been difficult, especially taking her from three loving children.

Michael went up to visit Neil and his staff. He was told they were winding down the collecting of the receivables, and they were almost whole in paying people back. Neil said that if they had the money Gail diverted from the company, they might even have a small surplus. Michael thanked them for their support and fairness. He asked what happened to Gail. Neil smiled, telling Michael she tried to get her license back to be an agent and the union unanimously denied her.

Michael started to plan to come back to New York. There was a bus stop around the corner from his house. Michael would love to sit on the bench and just zone out. He would try to connect the lines of what had happened and why people wanted him to burn. He realized he represented so much of the anxiety of what is disliked in the business. He could understand these feelings that existed in people, especially artists. So, Michael took the punishment. But due to Gail's actions, and some other selfish people, the innocent people that got punished most were the actors due to the loss of momentum on their careers. No one said, "Do not do this, the actors will lose." In Gail's amateur scheme, which all depended on eliminating Michael, she did not make provisions to help support the actors.

Michael got a call. Joe died. "No more. Please." Michael said, getting off the phone.

He went to the wake. He did not know Joe was local. There were lots of family and friends at the funeral home. Joe's mother came up to Michael, held his arm very tightly, and thanked him over and over.

She said, "You gave my son a chance, a sense of hope."

All Joe's brothers and sisters came over and hugged Michael. As he was leaving, Joe's father, looking awfully bad, shook Michael's hand saying, "You are okay, Michael. You cared for Joey. He would always talk about you and your kindness."

Michael said, "I appreciate that, but it was your son who saved me with the courage to tell the truth. So, I say thank you for your son."

Michael kissed Joe's mother on the cheek and left. As he stood on the street, he thought of how many friends he left behind, with some never saying goodbye. Most of them never had the chance to genuinely love and be loved.

Michael was going to stay in his sister's apartment in Brooklyn. It was large and perfect for the three of them. Everyone was packed and ready to go. They got on the 405 North, saying goodbye to LA. They must have been only two hours into the trip when the phone rang, and it was someone who worked for his friend Stanley, who was a very respected casting director. Stanley died that morning from sceptic poisoning while being operated on for an infection in his colon.

Michael was just devastated. "Oh God, not Stanley."

Stanley was Michael's best friend; they would go to the Rose Bowl flea market every Sunday and meet up for a drink at least once a week. Before Michael left, he and Stanley had a great dinner and four or five Martinis. When they came out of the restaurant, Michael told Stanley he would drive him home, but Stanley wanted to walk. The last image Michael had of him was Stanley walking up the side street of the restaurant, disappearing into the LA mist.

Michael's friend had bought a building in the city and invited Michael to take one of the lofts. The bigger bonus was the school district was one of the best in the city. Michael was extremely excited about this apartment; he would only have to live at his sister's apartment for a few months. The children and Michael drove cross country following Interstate 80, the northern route, which was breathtaking.

298

Since the children saw so much of the southern part of the West, which was I-10, it was a new experience for them. They loved the trip. They took fifteen days to get to New York, but they had so much fun driving and seeing great sights from the Grand Tetons, the Rockies, and the Western Plains.

They got into Scranton, Pennsylvania, and Michael told them, "Finally, we are there. Well guys," Michael said, "here is to a better life filled with new adventures."

CHAPTER TWENTY

2000-2004

Michael entered New York City, stopping at the approach to the Brooklyn Bridge to tell his little knights the crusade was over. They triumphantly crossed over the river to relish in their new beginning. They reached Michael's sister's house, unpacked, and slept. They did not wake up until the next morning. Michael got them ready to have breakfast. Michael explained that they were not the only people living in the house. The bottom floor was the office of a state senator and a representative for Brooklyn.

"We must lighten our load coming into the house and walking upstairs. We must not be noisy," said Michael.

After questioning Michael about the people on the bottom floor, the children agreed it was important to be quiet. Michael also told them they were friends of President Clinton—but not close friends.

Michael took the children into Manhattan to meet a friend who had the apartment for rent. He was shocked to find that they had just bought the house, but the tenants in the house were going nowhere. One of the primary reasons Michael came east was because of this apartment and the school district. This delay would cause problems. At the urging of his friends who owned the house, Michael was assured he could use the house address to get his kids into the district school.

Michael did ask, "What if the tenant stays and refuses to leave?"

"No way. The apartment is yours," his friend responded.

Michael went to the school the next day. The administrators at the school were very suspicious. He had to get some paperwork and prove he lived at that apartment. Michael fulfilled all their requests, and the children got into the school.

Michael realized something important, he did not come here to start living lies. He wanted freedom and to be truthful. Michael decided that this apartment was not for him. If he was going to make this future work, he and the children would do it on their own. Michael forgot how easy LA was compared to New York. Everything you do in New York was based on a quest to survive, but it was all going to happen on Michael's terms.

Michael was defining his human condition, looking at the key events in his life that made up his emotions, his goals, his conflicts, and most importantly, his mortality. Michael thought he was in great shape, spiritually; he was slowing embracing the Hindu philosophy. His goals were peace and his children's success. He was always awkward around people who might know about the fall of the agency.

Michael learned as time went on to leave that luggage outside the door. Most of those people were not important in Michael's pursuit of his own personal truth and wellbeing. Michael was free and living in New York just like he was in the early part of his life. He was unable to convince people that he was betrayed by Gail, but it did not matter anymore.

Michael was hired to teach at two universities as well as one college and one junior college. Also, he got a surprise call from a popular casting director who asked him to represent her like he did in LA. More importantly, she was a friend who cared for him. Michael had immense respect for her as a professional and as a person. She was honest and giving. Michael now had a foundation of income, the college and representing the casting director. Michael decided to try his hand at management in the entertainment industry one more time, working from his loft in Tribeca, which his sister helped him rent. He did make two great friends, June who helped him in the office during his new unenthused attempt at management and Marie, who was just truly a friend. June was tough. She was Tina in "Tony and Tina's Wedding" off Broadway. Marie was from the same elk but not in your face. Michael made two important choices—he would be celibate and maintain his solitude. With these choices, he found great quiet hours to think and just be.

Joshua and Elizabeth were flourishing, and both were playing soccer. Joshua was doing well. Scholastically, they were like every third grader. Their Game Boys took precedent over homework, though their grades were good. Money was always an issue, but Michael's sister helped. And his other sister was incredibly supportive. Michael would take the kids to school and then go off to work.

It was primary day, and Michael had all the intentions of voting. He reached the playground on a beautiful day; the sun was strong but not hot. Elizabeth's class went into the school, but Joshua's teacher still had not shown up. Michael told Joshua he was going in to vote. He told Joshua to wait in the playground with his classmates until his teacher came.

As Michael was standing in line to vote, the building jumped. It felt like when a truck hit those large metal plates over the holes on Chambers Street. The voting machines fell over. Michael picked up the machine and still voted.

He went in the hallway; he saw Joshua standing at the front door. "Dad a plane hit the trade center." Michael assured him that a lot of small planes hit the towers.

"No, dad, it was a big plane."

Michael walked up to Joshua as he passed the principal's office, which had a huge picture window. The sight Michael saw was unbelievable. The tower was on fire, and he saw lots of paper falling from the building. He went up to Joshua, right in the doorway leading outside, and hugged him.

Outside, Michael and Joshua saw a few people fall from the tower. He grabbed Joshua and went back in the school to get Elizabeth. It seemed like hours before she came down from her class. The principal closed the blinds facing the tower and came to Michael, telling him to leave and go home.

Elizabeth finally came down to the main floor, and they left the building. Suddenly, as they stood in front of the main door of the school, a huge fire ball appeared to fall from the Trade Center, they were only two blocks from the Trade Center. It was a second plane that hit the other tower. Michael grabbed both their hands and quickly began to move down the street, but the crowd in front of them was large and panicked. Suddenly, Elizabeth lost her grip on his hand, and Michael watched her be trampled by five grown men. Michael pushed them away, grabbed Elizabeth, and walked swiftly with them to the subway.

They decided to go to Grandma's and got a train to Brooklyn. But the train came to a halt at the first stop in downtown Brooklyn, and they had to get off. They walked upstairs, and a white cloud of dust came down like a snowstorm. Michael was nervous that a nuclear bomb went off. They continued to walk, and someone who was listening to a radio told them the south tower came down and fell toward Brooklyn.

Finally, they saw a bus. Michael did not care where the bus was going. To his disappointment, the bus only went two stops. They had to get off. Michael was determined to walk if he had to. The white dust got worse. One older man was handing out masks. For whatever reason, the gentlemen did not give one to Michael and the kids.

They were maskless, walking for about two miles attempting to hitch a ride. No one would pick them up. Suddenly, an African American reporter from a local newspaper generously stopped for them, and they made it to Grandma's.

The world stopped. Michael could never have imagined what he saw. But what about Joshua; he saw everything? He told Michael he saw the people in the plane as it flew over the school. It was low. Joshua developed fungal alopecia, and the WTC Fund paid for a psychiatrist for Joshua. Elizabeth was badly scarred on her arms from being trampled. She did not want to go to therapy, and Michael respected her wishes.

Staying with Grandma for a few days, she tried to cook in her wheelchair and made her great sauce, meatballs, and a salad. The colleges were closed for the week. The kids' school had too much debris around the building. Ultimately, they were temporarily housed at a public school in the Village. In a few days they had to move to a closed Catholic School one block away.

For the next few months, nothing happened except people asking Michael what it was like. One evening, they all went down to the pier, found a bench, and just snuggled next to each other.

Michael said, "Let's move. This city is not as safe as one would think." The kids agreed, but they asked where they would go.

Michael said, "No problem! I have the answer—Montclair, New Jersey. They have this great progressive middle school even though it is New Jersey. God, I never thought I would live in New Jersey!"

Michael knew about this place because the Dukakis family lived there and ran the Whole Theatre Company. One of them suggested Montclair numerous times to Michael in the past. They then went to get pizza. The year was out, and the kids left an extremely competitive school with great grades. Elizabeth left behind friends, Joshua his first true love.

They rented a small but functionable apartment in Montclair. They wanted to slowly adapt to Montclair. The kids were admitted into the progressive middle school Michael wanted for them. They liked Montclair. It was funny—the more working-class people accepted Michael as a single parent, but the more affluent people had a tough time accepting Michael. But not the kids; they liked his children.

Michael thought they were expecting someone in tailored jeans who was a bit elitist. Michael was the Michael he always appeared to be—a bit rougher, forthrightly honest, proactive, and very opinionated. Michael was assured. He did not care what they thought and had no design to find a companion in Montclair. Michael and the children liked the town, and many people of the town were great. Michael was alone with the children and the dogs, but he was content.

One night, Michael got a call from Luke, a successful stage director. He invited Michael out for lunch. Michael instead invited him to his house, as it was too early to leave the security of his home. Luke wanted Michael to help him rewrite a script for a musical. Michael said no. He had a terrible situation in New York when he helped an old friend restructure a script. He did a fantastic job and got paid, but the friend wanted the money back and Michael refused. He took Michael to court. They never made it to the judge, and they both walked away.

After hearing this story, Luke said he would never do that to Michael, and it would be fun to work together. Michael agreed and Luke never stopped coming over to the house. They finally had a great script. Luke got two producers interested in the play. Michael thought he would be attached to the project.

Luke said, "Sure enough."

They set up a meeting with this gentleman in a bar/restaurant he owned. When Michael got there, he realized this gentleman was a Reservoir Man. But the meeting went well. Michael left Luke, who thanked him repeatedly for his help and involvement.

A few weeks went by, and Michael did not hear from Luke at all. Michael called Luke. Luke told him the producer did not hit it off with Michael and he would prefer for him not to be involved. Luke kept on saying he was sorry. Michael put down the phone and went back to the news. The play did open but failed. Michael said, "It is what it is."

They finally found a great house with three bedrooms, big back, and expansive front yard. Michael had a large office, and they also had a dining room, big living room, and a great kitchen. The day they moved in; Michael got a phone call. Susan had died. Michael was heartbroken. Susan was the best. She and Joe led him to a road of freedom, freeing him from the grips of his own despair and the Reservoir Men. Susan's death was unexpected and very emotional for Michael.

Michael decided to adopt another dog to keep Sandy, the family's old Labrador, company. They all went to a rescue pound and found what was to be Michael's charm. They adopted a Beagle and named him Buddy. Buddy's first weeks home were incredible. Michael and Buddy bonded like no other master and pet.

Michael was the leader of Buddy's pack, and Buddy would follow Michael everywhere. When Michael sat, Buddy sat right next to him. Buddy slept right next to Michael, and if he were a little insecure, he would cuddle even closer to him, with his back against Michael's leg.

As time passed, Michael realized that Buddy loved to listen to Edith Piaf while sitting on the couch next to Michael. When Michael left the house, Buddy would cry for a bit and then go to the couch to look out the window and wait for Michael to return. Buddy would protect Michael from all that corruption that surrounded him. It became the Michael and Buddy show, with Buddy protecting the Realm and the family.

Frances was getting bad, in and out of hospitals with no significant terminal diagnosis. Every visit to the hospital or to her apartment, Frances would put five dollars on the edge of the bed, telling Michael to get the children ice cream even if it was four degrees outside. She was going on ninety, and Michael sensed her time was near.

Michael would sit in Frances' room and stare at her, thanking her repeatedly in his mind. What a great life she and Andy gave to him. Somehow, she understood who the Reservoir Men were when Michael told her about them. Michael explained to Frances that when he was young, he would go up to the park and see the Reservoir Men walk aimlessly, waiting to be accepted.

Frances said, "You should not bother with them Michael. What good could they do for you?" Frances was unaware how many Reservoir Men Michael met during his life.

He told her out of nowhere, "I went on and forgot about them. All I wanted was peace and some form of communion with the beauty around me. I am okay now, Frances," said Michael.

Frances looked at him and said, "What did you call me? I am your mother! And I know you are okay; you are simply fine."

Michael was stunned. Imagine if she knew that Michael was calling her Frances in his head for years. Michael told her he was leaving. She asked him to turn on the TV so she could watch the Mexicans playing music with his father on the television. Michael was unfazed by the request. At least this time she forgot to offer ice cream in the dead of winter. Michael kissed Frances, turned on the TV, grabbed the kids, and left.

Time passed quickly; Michael loved sitting in the backyard. Sometimes he would reread some of his favorite novels. He was not interested in new writers, only those old masters who made Michael remember how inspired he felt when he first read their writings. Michael could not take off any weight with both diet and exercise. He was getting older and heavier but was still adventurous.

Occasionally, a few old friends would call him up and talk to him, often asking if he was with someone. "Besides Buddy, Sandy, and the children, no!" he said with a smile. "For the past nine years, I have been celibate."

Their reaction would be a laugh or a gentle, "No way, not you, Michael."

Michael would calmly say, "Why would I want someone to put in their two cents about the raising of my children and my dogs?"

He was happy alone watching everyone growing older. One thing Michael did do that gave him contentment was study Hinduism. It was the mantra and meditation that really got him hooked.

Michael started meditating every night. He had a great mantra: "Ra Ma Da Sa, Sa Say So Hung," meaning sun, moon, earth, infinity, all that is in my infinity, and I am Thou." Michael would do the mantra at least once a day. His back up mantra was "May the light of a thousand suns shine through. Live the life of Grace that you were meant to...and the pure light within you guide your way home." This enabled him to release so much of the bad energy he had maintained over the years. Buddy would sit right next to him while he meditated. Michael swore he was humming too.

CHAPTER TWENTY-ONE

2004-Yesterday

Michael picked up *The New York Times* as he did every day. He sat at the kitchen table with his coffee. He had a habit of checking the obituaries since the AIDS epidemic. To his shock, he read that Eliott, his old College Dean, had died. He died from complications of AIDS.

Michael had mixed feelings. He was happy he accepted his apology, but to erase the image he portrayed of Michael was hard to forget. What did he see in Michael? A cute, lower-class guy that he found attractive? A conquest? There was never a doubt in Michael's mind that Eliott was a Reservoir Man.

Michael was sure Eliott was enlisting him to join the flock of Reservoir Men. If Michael ever did, that action would have cost his freedom. He would just become part of the lost souls never truly finding themselves. Michael checked for any memorial services, as he felt he should go. He quickly changed his mind. The chapter with Eliott was over, but he was grateful for all he taught him about producing and the entertainment industry. The rest was better forgotten.

Michael wondered how younger men and women dealt with coming of age, with the pain in discovering their feelings and identity. Who do they turn to if anyone at all? How many scars would they take into adulthood and what effects would those scars have throughout their lives? Who were their Reservoir Men? A friend, a relative, a parent, or a teacher ready to reject or use them? Hopefully, there was someone out there to show them the light shining through, like a thousand rays of the sun, illuminating their beliefs in themselves for the world around them to see.

June and Marie stopped by the house and asked Michael out for a drink and a few laughs. Michael had a wonderful time, as he usually did with June and Marie. They came back to the house and played with Buddy and forgot about Michael; Buddy needed some love anyway. They were about to leave when Marie told Michael that she would be going into the hospital for a small procedure and that her boyfriend would keep everyone posted. They all kissed, and June told Michael she was so happy that he seemed so content.

Two days passed; Michael got a phone call that Marie passed away from sceptic poisoning at the hospital. Michael left the room when he received the call, went upstairs, and meditated. Michael loved Marie.

Michael was curious why, with all the deaths from AIDS, there was not a national memorial, except for two small memorials in New York and San Francesco. The quilt was locked up in a warehouse, taken out in pieces to be exhibited occasionally. Those 700,000 people who had died from AIDS and suffered unmercifully agonizing deaths deserved something. They were sons, brothers, and friends. But where could one go to honor them?

Michael thought about all the art, educators, chefs, actors, directors, and politicians that would have made our lives so much richer. What about the ordinary guy who could give someone love where none existed? "We missed a lot," thought Michael to himself. He would have loved to go somewhere peaceful, to spend moments, hours, days thinking about those he lost.

Michael's relationship with Joshua and Elizabeth was great through the early years of high school. They would always go to the movies or out to dinner. Michael was incredibly involved in their school projects. Joshua excelled in baseball; Elizabeth lost interest in sports but became increasingly involved in social justice. Her paintings were becoming exceptional. Elizabeth was asked by the high school principal to paint a mural on the second floor of the building. The mural was on the activists of the 1960s and their commitment to social justice. The mural filled one third of the hall. What an accomplishment.

Joshua left baseball. He found the team members too concerned with their own achievements and not with the team's effort. Joshua believed the coach was too concerned with keeping his job, which he demonstrated by being very nasty to the members of the team. He was portraying the myth of the angry coach, which was not valuable to a young team's success.

Michael was in Manhattan dropping off a contract on behalf of his client. He was stopped by an old acquaintance from LA, Tom, going down the subway stairs. Tom asked Michael to grab a cup of coffee and catch up. Michael was not anxious to have coffee. He did not want to talk about what happened in LA. Tom seemed to want to talk about something other than gossip. Tom had a project, an off-Broadway show about two conjoined twins—one gay and the other straight. Michael agreed to read it. Michael asked Tom how he was doing. Tom explained he had problems that he did not want to discuss as they were too personal.

Finally, Tom asked Michael how he was and what happened in LA. Tom thought he got a raw deal, and he believed that it was all Gail's doing. Michael smiled and told Tom he did not want to talk about what happened. He and the children were simply fine. Michael took the script, his phone number, and told Tom to give him a week. As they parted, Michael knew Tom was a Reservoir Man. Unless the script was great, he would pass on the project.

Michael read the script and found it very funny. He wondered what luggage he would have to bear from Tom. Michael was not interested in Tom's personal life, just the work. He called Tom, asking him what he wanted Michael to do on the project.

Tom told Michael, "I just need a guide, someone to help me do the right things." Tom then told Michael they were to be part of a major off-

Broadway "new play" festival. Michael asked Tom if there was money involved. Michael knew the answer already.

"Not right now, but I will make sure you get a good amount when the play opens."

Michael knew what that meant but he proceeded. Tom threw a carrot to Michael, getting Joshua and Elizabeth a job running crew for all the plays in a summer play festival—with pay. Michael felt that the kids seeing how a professional play was run would be good for them.

Tom said, "If you have notes on the script, email them. I need you to come to all four performances at the festival." Of course, Michael would be there anyway since he had to take Joshua and Elizabeth back and forth from the city.

Michael worked on the play and cleaned up the script for Tom. The group around the production started to grow and glow with the possibility of the play's success. Tom found an investor, and Michael asked him for a contract and a guarantee for Michael's investment of his time working on the play. Tom agreed and then drew up a badly worded contract. Michael just wanted his signature.

The group had a meeting set up in the city at the Plaza Hotel with the man who was going to sign the check, green lighting the entire project. The day of the meeting, Michael had a flu-like sickness but still went. The numbers Tom presented to the guy were all inaccurate. Michael pointed out two big misconceptions in their approach in producing the play during the meeting. Tom just glared at Michael. They finished the meeting, and they all left.

A week later, Tom called Michael to tell him that Tom was out as one of the producers and given "a diminished role as a writer." Michael quickly asked about their agreement. Tom said he would fight for Michael to get everything he should get. Michael never received a penny. The play opened with complimentary reviews, but no one came to see it.

They closed in a few months. "These parasites come in so many forms. I am done with all these Reservoir Men; I feel stripped of my self-respect and my intellectual integrity."

In the end, it was Michael's fault as well; he felt for these people who needed help. Consciously, Michael knew these people were the misfits of the entertainment industry. They did not understand how harmful their misguided wants were, not only to Michael, but to themselves and to anyone who met them.

Michael had learned something; it was an important truth these people would never learn. Dreams, when they come to you, are pure. You must grab them, hold tight, and invite as few people as possible in their development. When they come alive, only then, can you share them with everyone. After that phone call, Michael went to his couch and held Buddy on his lap. It was his dream to have a life without any Reservoir Men. It was him and Buddy alone.

Michael still had the need to confront Ben from Dover and say sorry. Since Michael had last seen him, Ben started a successful lighting design company in Albany. After finding his number online, Michael decided to call Ben at his home. Michael would pose as a potential client asking for advice on lighting without divulging who he was. Michael called only to find out Ben retired.

"How old are you?" asked Michael.

"Fifty-six," said Ben.

"Retired? At fifty-six? So early in your career?" asked Michael.

"It was time," said Ben. Michael realized Ben knew it was him on the phone. Michael felt foolish calling thirty years later. So, Michael said good-bye and hung up.

Michael was now seeing the pattern. He sought help or people sought help from him until it all went up in flames. Michael was the most successful when he did things on his own. He remembered the Reservoir Man who followed him to his house and then to his sister's. Michael almost let him into the house. What would have happened to Michael if he let him in? How would he have changed? Michael knew that the Reservoir Man could never enter his house. It was important to keep him outside.

In his house now, it was quiet; it was solitude and freedom. In his house, it was Joshua, Elizabeth, and Buddy. It was his own choices, as imperfect as they might were. It was his imperfect house, and no one could enter it to burn it down.

Even with the mistakes and the problems, Michael worked hard in attempting to keep the business of his life going. He was holding Buddy and looking through the window seeing a Reservoir Man. He did not hate him; he did not hate any of the Reservoir Men. In fact, he understood their

322

pain and recognized their human condition. Michael understood who the man was—he was Michael if he made all the wrong choices, did all the wrong things, and listened to all the wrong people. It was Michael's choices and his principles now that built him this house, this family, and this freedom. He would never let them take it away.

Graduation day was here. Everyone was excited. Michael planned a nice dinner after graduation. Joshua and Elizabeth invited a few friends that were not graduating yet. Joshua graduated with high honors and Elizabeth was recognized for all her artwork, especially the mural. Both children were going to great universities in New Jersey. Joshua wanted to major in History and Music. Elizabeth was to major in Art, so she entered a BFA program.

Joshua and Elizabeth got lots of gifts from family and friends. Michael told them they could spend half of it, and the other half should be put away in savings. His generosity was because Elizabeth was on full scholarship and Joshua mostly on a full scholarship. Since Joshua was going to a Catholic university, it was expensive. The summer before college was great. Peace prevailed over Michael and his home as it did for the last eight years.

Michael made friends with a great guy; they drank a lot together. Bob was a bit mysterious; Michael knew nothing of his past, or for that matter, his present. He also did not know where Bob lived. Bob would come over every night, stay late, then disappear into the night. Michael liked this, but time wore on the friendship.

They drew apart—with no anxiety or anger. Bob was not a Reservoir Man. He knew who he was. They would often talk about these abstract feelings and objectives. Michael learned a lot from Bob, even though he was twenty years younger. They were on equal terms, respecting each other and feeling for each other. Bob left one night and did not return. Michael did get a DVD mailed to him from Bob titled "Moulin Rouge." Michael loved this film. As soon as he got it, he placed it into his DVD player, playing it repeatedly.

Michael's sister called. Frances was going back to the hospital, but it did not look good. Michael got into his car and drove to Brooklyn with Elizabeth. Elizabeth was close to Frances, as was Joshua. Elizabeth liked brushing her hair and making her look pretty. Michael and Elizabeth sat in her room alone. She had the hospital room to herself; it was a private room. She was conscious and happy to see Elizabeth. She asked for Joshua because she wanted to see him. Michael told her he would bring him tomorrow.

They had a nice visit. Frances told them that her brother-in-law, Walter, had all her jewelry. Frances had a lot of expensive jewelry. Every time she went into the hospital, Walter got the jewelry. He always rode in the ambulance with her. As they were leaving the hospital room, Michael made Frances laugh. At the door was his sister, she wanted to know why Michael did not tell her he was coming to the hospital. Michael said he never gave it a thought.

"She is extremely sick. Glad you came," his sister said.

The next night there were bad storms both in New York and New Jersey. Michael's sister called, and told Michael that Frances was going to pass. Michael told her he would be right there. She told him to stay home. Michael would never understand why she told him not to come.

Frances passed away late that night. Michael was devastated. He did not get to say goodbye. He put Elizabeth and Joshua in the car and left for Brooklyn. When they got to the hospital, they had already taken Frances to the morgue. Michael pleaded with the staff to see her one last time. They agreed, but the children could not go.

Michael made it down to the morgue. She was not put away into the drawers yet. Michael looked at her, said goodbye, and kissed her forehead. She looked so peaceful. Her face resembled the day in the limousine when Andy died, and she wore a black veil. She looked so young, like a bride.

"Frances, you were the best combo. Andy and Frances were great together. Thank you for all you did." Michael lost a major connector to the links of his life.

Frances' wake was full of flowers and mass cards. Michael walked around like a lost puppy. The amount of people who came up to him and gave condolences was overwhelming. After everyone went home, Michael sat with Joshua and Elizabeth right next to the coffin and stared at Frances.

"Oh God, I wish I would have spent more time with you and Andy. We would have gone on so many trips!"

All three of them sat in silence until the funeral director came over asking them to leave. As they were driving home, they passed a Chinese restaurant. Michael pulled up. They got out and ordered all of Frances' favorite foods. They laughed and talked about all the enjoyable times they had with Frances.

The second night was the Rosary. A lot more people came, and the wake started to get a party attitude. People were catching up, especially those who had not seen each other in a long time. Poor Frances. She could not partake in any of the conversation. Michael's young cousin came over to him, asking Michael if he remembered telling him that "men do not cry" at Andy's wake.

Michael answered, "They don't. End of conversation."

The next morning was the funeral. They had a long drive to the cemetery. There were six limousines and four flower cars. They got to the cemetery, and she had a nice burial.

As they were leaving, Frances' brother asked, "Are we all going to eat?"

Michael's sister did not answer. Frances's brother, in anger said, "This is the way you are burying my sister? Not having a lunch and being together as a family?"

Michael's older sister said, "Come over to my daughter's house. We will order pizza."

His younger sister planned everything but no celebration of her life. Michael would never forget this; he had no idea why this happened, but he had to assume some of the blame. He could have been more involved. What a disgrace to a wonderful woman. He and the children drove home. Michael was happy he had Chinese food the night before, a last night in honor of Frances.

It was hard for Michael to concentrate after Frances' death. He was teaching six classes a week at the colleges. He was able to use his extra time outside of the classroom to unleash his anxiety over the death of Frances. One other thing that kept his mind off Frances' death and funeral was Buddy. Buddy loved to play with Michael.

At midday, Michael would give him a big bone. The bones were bigger than Buddy's jaw. He would hold it in his mouth until Michael would say, "Give me the bone!"

Forcing both to run around the house. If Michael caught Buddy in a room, he would say, "Give me the bone!"

Buddy would growl so loud that anyone would think he was going to bite. This was a daily episode. Buddy would love to eat his dry food on the couch with a hand towel holding the food. Michael would attempt to steal the food, and Buddy would lightly bite back. If they did not play this game, Buddy would not eat. The games went on and on, by Buddy's rules.

Joshua came home from college and told Michael he saw the best thing—a house on the river all alone with no other houses next door. He asked Michael if they could check it out.

"Sure, I was getting tired of Montclair," said Michael.

That same afternoon, Elizabeth told Michael she was dropping out of college and moving to Boston with her boyfriend. The art professors did not understand her or her approach to art. Michael had to respect what she decided. One day, she might change her mind.

"Okay, brother, let's check this house out," said Michael to Joshua.

The house was in Little Falls, a bedroom community of Montclair. They got to the house, and Michael was impressed. The entire backyard was on the river. Though it was smaller than they were used to, it did have three bedrooms in case Elizabeth returned from Boston. They were told by a gentleman across the street that the fishing was great in the summer. There was no real estate broker, which made it a little more attractive.

So, Michael signed the lease, and they moved in. Joshua fished and fished, but the deal Michael had with Joshua was that Joshua threw the fish back in the river. Michael did not eat fish and would not cook them anyway. Michael had been a vegetarian or a partial vegetarian since he was twenty-eight, fish was off the menu.

November proved to be a rainy month, and suddenly, the backyard was covered with about three feet of water. The press came knocking on his door, asking him how worried he was about the possibility for a large flood. Michael was sure it would recede into the river, and it did. The spring brought more rain, and the river in the backyard was a bit higher this time. The geese were swimming outside Michael's bedroom window and even pecking on the window.

The summer came. It was hot and rainy, but there were no floods in the yard. The summer was ending, and hurricane Irene was coming up the coast. Irene's rain was so bad that when it stopped, the anticipated flood came. They had about a foot of water in the house, but they protected their furniture and art. The city housed them in a shelter located in Little Falls. Michael bought a queen blow up bed. He did not want to sleep on a cot.

Michael and Joshua lived in the shelter for five days. The water was receding from the houses and the street. They closed the shelter. Michael and Joshua had nowhere to live since most of the family lived in Long Island.

Buddy was staying at a friend's small apartment, wondering when he was going to play the bone game again. They slept in the car at the parking lot of the shelter.

The second night, the rain came back. It was another hurricane— Lee. The shelter reopened within two days, and their home was destroyed. The water was over the windows. It was so bad that it made the national news. Michael sat down with FEMA. Even though he did not own the house, he was eligible for aide.

Joshua said to Michael, "I am so sorry. It was a bad idea to move here."

Michael said as he kissed his head, "Forget about it. We will have a new adventure." They both laughed.

"Let's get some pizza," Joshua said to Michael.

FEMA found a house for Michael. It was big with three bedrooms and two dens, and the government would pay the rent up to $1,500 for eight months. They gave him an allowance to buy unused furniture, clothes, and groceries. This was a small constellation for the memories Michael lost during the flood. But the children's photos and their memorabilia, including Elizabeth's canvasses, were saved.

FEMA was the best; they moved Michael to a new rental home, which had plenty of back yard as well as the front. Michael and Joshua worked hard in getting the house together. Two days living at the house, who knocks on the door and walks into the living room? Elizabeth. She was thinking of moving in.

"Sure, great," said Michael, "When do you think you will?"

Elizabeth said, "Now. I have my things in Chris' car."

Elizabeth slept on the floor with Chris, her boyfriend. They all had fun, and Michael had two extra hands in fixing up the house. This was short lived. Elizabeth was going to live with Chris' mother two towns over. Michael kept asking her if she thought it was really a good idea. Elizabeth thought it was brilliant, and it all seemed to work out.

Joshua graduated from college with honors. Michael thought, "What are we going to do with a Music/History degree?"

Michael thought the same in reference to his own college career. He had three majors for his BA than the MFA. Michael told Joshua, "Start your own business. Make your own way."

One week after Joshua's graduation, Michael was given devastating news that his best friend Robert died from a heart attack. Robert was involved in Michael's life since Dover, where he was a member of Michael's acting company. Robert was not part of a larger group of friends, but instead stood alone in his friendship with Michael.

During Michael's troubles in LA, Robert would defend Michael many times amongst people who were so willing to condemn him. Robert was, in Michael's eyes, one of the best African American actors to ever perform Shakespeare. Michael would miss Robert's weekly phone calls where, as the years went on, Michael would consistently enjoy Robert singing "Ol' Man River" from "Show Boat" to Michael over the phone as they both enjoyed a great laugh together. Michael at times would sing back Thelma Houston's "Don't Leave Me This Way." Robert was a great friend.

Michael had a student, Jason, in one of his classes who was Italian, but you would not believe it seeing him. His costume was authentic, cut off sleeves but skinny arms, jeans, and if you listened closely, you would detect a slight Brooklyn accent.

One day, he walked up to Michael and said, "You remind me of myself."

Michael's response was, "Great." But in his mind, he thought, "No way, brother. You are not like me."

Michael invited him for coffee at the school café to discuss his career objectives in the entertainment business. They met and hit it off. During subsequent meetings, Michael read his journal and was extremely impressed with how he viewed things around him and the universe. He told Michael he was in the business school and minoring in film. He was taking business as a major

334

so he could produce films for his brother, who recently graduated from a well know film school.

Michael said to him, "Produce for yourself. Change your major to film and rush your graduation to three years. You get corrupted in film school to one degree or another. Most professors are not practitioners. They never do any professional work. They only observe. What do they know? Search for your own self or truth. There, you will find all your answers. Just do it! And even if you do not hit the top, you will hit something and be content. You must be satisfied then with yourself."

Michel invited Jason over to the house, and as time wore on, he moved in and developed a strong professional friendship with Joshua. Joshua and Jason formed a film company, with Michael helping them. In eight years, they produced seventeen award-winning short films, two documentaries, and four feature films with major distribution—making money. As for Elizabeth, she had a beautiful baby girl.

Chris' mother was exceedingly kind and told Elizabeth she could still live with them and would be incredibly happy helping her raise the baby. Michael now had order in his universe. Michael enjoyed being with Joshua and Jason. They had fun making films, and Michael loved watching his daughter raise his grandchild. This was the happiest Michael was for a long time, maybe since he was running his theatre in upstate New York.

Michael was determined to lose lots of weight. He was starting to take pride in himself again. His health was great—a couple of bumps, nothing more. He was immensely proud of his health. Sandy had passed away a year ago, and Buddy was getting old. Michael tried to make friends, occasionally, but could not maintain the friendships.

Michael did not like to talk, but instead sit still and observe things around him, just like when he went to the park and sat on the benches as a young man. He would often think of Maritzo and the two wonderful nights where he touched his soul, making him whole for that moment. He helped Michael find goodness, showing him that he needed to see the real world and not just the shadows on the wall.

Claire gave Michael the warmth, companionship, and the tenderness of a woman. It might have been great spending a longer time with her. Then there was Adriano, who was able to shed and share his handicap, for a brief night. Ben, Michael's master electrian, the most honest young man he ever knew. Ben saw Michael's truth, in an innocent way. Ben always pointed out to Michael the goodness he saw in him.

How about all the other people that just walked by Michael that he did not notice? How about all the dead friends and acquaintances he never said goodbye to, especially Frances, Susan, Stanley, Robert, and Joe? Michael was able to reminisce about the times they all had together, and he missed them so painfully.

Joshua stayed by him and had unconditional love toward him. Michael would love when Joshua would go shopping with him and pick out his clothes. Joshua was a friend and a son. Jason was a great friend, generous with his time and caring. Elizabeth gave him a beautiful granddaughter, and hopefully, would recapture her art. With all her bravado, she was a wonderful daughter.

Michael would always tell Joshua and Elizabeth, "Find your truth, look deep into yourself, and when you understand what is there, you will see that man is inherently good; what your truth is, that is what makes you, you! Joshua, Elizabeth, see the goodness in yourself, not a religious type of goodness but the embodiment of love, giving, and caring." Michael survived; Michael can now breathe; he can see the ends of all the roads in his life coming together.

Michael would love to go to the river with Buddy and sit on the bench. He would always remember what Heraclitus, the Greek philosopher, said about the river: everything is constantly changing. Like life, the river changes. Like Michael's life, it would always be changing. We are all in this state of flux. We will never see the same part of the river twice. Our moments pass by and quickly become memories.

Buddy might have understood this because he just sat there on Michael's lap, staring at him. Michael became increasingly introverted. He stayed away from his extended family, except for one niece and nephew. His family always acted as if he came from Mars or somewhere else.

Joshua and Jason helped Michael quite a bit since his knee was bad and he had a lumbar problem. But the doctors promised a procedure would clear the back all up. Buddy was the man; Michael would wrap his arms around him at night and go under the bed spread, holding on to him tightly while they each fell asleep. Buddy was getting so old and sickly; Michael would have to carry him everywhere.

It was a lovely day, Michael got Buddy, put him in the car and drove to the bench by the river. They got to their bench; some children were playing. Michael said to himself "No Reservoir Men, great." As he smiled at the thought.

Buddy cuddled in his lap as Michael pet him. Michael whispered to Buddy, "You know, freedom has a price but the result for me...I didn't need anyone but myself in the end, maybe except you and the children."

Michael went deep in thought; he finally went to adjust Buddy on his lap, who felt heavy. As he looked down, he noticed Buddy was not moving. Michael realized Buddy had left him but here he was all the same, the warmth of his body still there but even that was fading now. The sun was lowering, and the trees grew dark, but Michael sat with Buddy and watched as all the water passed and changed and never stopped.

In the darkness of the twilight, one could see a man with his Dog who was crying, and the faint whisper of his last goodbye to his best-friend and to his life as it was in the river of changing lives, people, and places.

You could hear Michael whimper, but it was the realization that was the most resounding, he said, alone but fulfilled, "Men do cry."

***

Non, je ne regrette rien

Made in United States
Orlando, FL
10 September 2022